LUCKY JONAH

LUCKY
JONAH

Richard Scrimger

HarperTrophyCanada

Lucky Jonah
Copyright © 2016 by Richard Scrimger.
All rights reserved.

Published by Harper*Trophy*Canada™, an imprint of HarperCollins Publishers Ltd

First edition

Harper*Trophy*Canada™ is a trademark of HarperCollins Publishers Ltd

HarperCollins books may be purchased for educational, business,
or sales promotional use through our Special Markets Department.

HarperCollins Publishers Ltd
2 Bloor Street East, 20th Floor
Toronto, Ontario, Canada
M4W 1A8

www.harpercollins.ca

Library and Archives Canada Cataloguing in Publication
information is available upon request.

ISBN 978-144341-071-7

Printed and bound in the United States
RRD 9 8 7 6 5 4 3 2 1

In memory of Thos Suddon and Guy Dubois

Perhaps I am stronger than I think.
—Thomas Merton

And I'm not anything that you think I am anyway.
—Syd Barrett

CHAPTER 1

The jump shot goes up. Looks good to me, but what do I know? I don't play basketball. I'm watching from the sidelines.

The shot doesn't look good to my friend Magnus.

"Short!" he calls. He works his way towards the basket and leaps at just the right time to grab the rebound.

"Back to me!" calls the shooter, a guy with dyed blond hair on Magnus's team.

Magnus fakes the pass, spins, and drives to the basket, beating an enormously tall, skinny guy named McClarty, who plays for the East High School team. McClarty looks like a line segment—length without breadth—but does he ever have length! He has to duck through doors. Magnus beats him, though, and his layup drops through the chain netting for an easy two points. McClarty shakes his head in frustration.

Lisa screams, "Yay, Magnus!" in my ear.

I am aware of throbbing in my right cheek—the one on my face. My butt cheeks are fine. I'm sitting on them, on a cement bench next to the public basketball court in Peace

Park in Dresden, Ontario, my small town, on a warm September Saturday. Sun's out for a change after a wet, grey week. The park is busy in a relaxed way—Frisbees, dogs, baby strollers on their way to and from the Dresden Mall. Traffic glides along Elgin Street, maybe going to the mall, but in no particular hurry to get there, or to the gas station or the building supply store or the Golden Years Villa, where my nana lives. Away over the hill and past the subdivisions, the hum of the highway coats this and every other moment of my life.

Magnus trots backwards, his muscles sliding under his tight skin. His hair floats like whipped cream on a milkshake.

"Isn't he great?" says Lisa.

He slaps hands with his teammates but keeps his eyes up-court the whole time.

"He's even better than those high school kids. Don't you think so, Jonah?"

"He's kind of perfect," I say.

"Don't you wish you could play like him?"

"Play like him? I wish I could be him."

I'm trying for funny here, but it comes out weird. Lisa gives me a look, slides away from me down the bench, turns back to the game.

I sigh. This is turning out to be a terrible day.

The yuckiness began a couple of hours ago, when I woke up with a throbbing that started at my neck and went all the way to the ends of my hair. I staggered to the bathroom and discovered an enormous zit forming on my left cheek.

Eek. Yikes. Oh my. All that kind of stuff.

I shouldn't have zits. I'm too young. Too cute. Other people have zits, and I'm not like them. My big brother has zits, and I'm sure not like him! But there it was, huge and shiny, as hard to ignore as a full moon. I got dressed and came downstairs, cautiously. My cheek hurt with every step. Ray pointed and burst out laughing.

"Shut up, Ray! You have zits too."

"My little brother is finally growing up. Soon you'll get a deeper voice, eh?"

He made his voice drop halfway through the word, so it came out "Eh-*ehh.*"

He laughed some more.

My voice has started to do that, and Ray finds it hilarious. He doesn't beat me up, but he's a bully, all right. My brother, the bully. He's two years older, in grade ten. I'm not looking forward to being in the same school as him next year.

He ran through the kitchen, pushing the swing door hard enough to bang against the wall. Ray runs everywhere—to school or corner store, mall or park, upstairs or down. He's been running even more than usual this last month, training for tomorrow's marathon. He's got enough energy for both of us. He may have enough for everyone on the planet.

I dropped a bagel in the toaster and tried to block him out of my mind.

Mom came up from the basement with a basket of clean laundry and a smile as wide as a barn door.

"Morning, morning, morning!" she said.

She's like that. She can sound enthusiastic about, I don't know, dust.

"Morning," I said.

"Isn't it beautiful, Jonah? A sunny fall day is my favourite day of the year. The air is fresh. The flowers are bright. And the birds are singing like . . . like . . ."

I helped her out. "Like birds," I said.

She laughed, *haw haw*, and tilted her head to one side.

"Are you all right, dear? You don't look like your regular self. You look—"

"Different?" I said.

She went *haw haw* again. Seriously, that's how she laughs—like a goose honking. You can hear it across the road. It's kind of adorable.

"I'm not different," I said. "Unless you mean this—" I pointed to my cheek.

"Oh, that!" she said. "That'll go away."

She took the basket of laundry upstairs, humming a happy tune. Good old Mom.

After breakfast I went out to the backyard. My father and brother stood side by side, raking grass clippings into piles. Dad asked me to grab a rake and help them neaten up the lawn.

Ray gave something between a sneer and a laugh—a snuff.

"*Neaten up?* Jonah? Dad, look at him. We don't need him to help us neaten things up. We don't want him."

"Now, Ray. You just ease up on your brother there."

"He's the one easing up, Dad. Am I right? Look at those pants. Those are some relaxed pants."

Ray wore a tight-fitting T-shirt and running shorts, both made out of a miracle material that wicks away sweat and weighs less than nothing. Not me. My clothes bagged on me, hung down, didn't match. I was casual. Maybe a bit sloppy. Okay, maybe a lot.

"Most people dress for success," said Ray. "But not Jonah. Jonah dresses for failure. Aren't I right, Dad?"

"Now, now," said Dad.

That was how it usually went. Ray teased me, and Dad went "Tsk, tsk" or "Hey, now." You can't pick your family, but sometimes I wish I could trade mine in. I've stuck with them for thirteen years now—I should be due for an upgrade.

Magnus lives a few blocks away. A fire truck was backing down his driveway as I was walking up. Dresden has a volunteer department, and Magnus's dad is a captain. Mr. Quinn must have popped home to get something. He waved to me from behind the wheel. The truck rumbled and dieselled down the street, trailing puffs of smoke.

Mrs. Quinn answered the door in her tennis shoes and concerned face. She told me that Magnus had gone to Peace Park to play basketball.

"*So sorry* you missed him, Jonah," she said.

That's one of her phrases. *So sorry.* So sorry you failed the test. So sorry you didn't make the team. So sorry to hear about your chicken pox, your crummy summer vacation, your life. So sorry for you.

"Lisa Van der Plotz went with Magnus," she said. "Do you know Lisa?"

Dresden is a small town. I've known Lisa since

kindergarten. She and Magnus and I are in the same math class now. His mom was aware of this. She was just being—I don't know what she was being.

"Such a nice girl, don't you think? And so well dressed. A gold necklace on a Saturday morning! I'm glad she and Magnus are friends. You could learn from her, Jonah. It wouldn't hurt you to dress nicer. And her skin is so clean too."

She frowned at my cheek and then at my baggy pants, and she closed the door.

On my way up Burnham Street, I saw a delivery truck parked in front of the Elegrooter place and a guy from the store driving a new power mower down the ramp. Old Elegrooter watched from the sidewalk with his thumbs hooked in his belt, beaming like a, like a light bulb. A couple doors away, a little kid in a Red Wings jersey stick-handled a tennis ball up his driveway, deking an imaginary goal-tender to score on an empty net. When he jumped in the air to celebrate, his bangs flopped over his eyes. He was having as much fun as a kitten with a piece of string.

I found a piece of gum in my pocket, but it hurt my cheek to chew, so I spat it out. I made my way slowly over to Westwood Avenue and followed it to Peace Park.

CHAPTER 2

And here I sit on the end of a wood and concrete bench, my left cheek a-throb, bored and angry and sorry for myself. It's not just Ray, and Lisa, and Magnus's mom. There's more wrong with my life than them. It's, it's like, it's *me* too. Something different about me, and more important than the zit. I feel something hanging over me—something grey and heavy, like a storm cloud. It's been building for a while. I kind of know what it is. But I don't want to look up. Maybe if I don't look up, it won't rain.

The ball bounces away from a kid with the name *GUS* shaved into his short haircut. He charges after the ball, trying to save it before it goes out of bounds. He misses, stumbles, and loses his balance, falling towards me on the bench. His hands are outstretched, his eyes wide and staring.

All the clocks slow down, and the scene unfolds in my mind. I get these visions now and then—things that are going to happen. A few years ago, Nana took me and Ray to a Raptors game. We went by subway. They stopped to buy candy, and I was alone on the platform for a few minutes. I had this vivid picture of the two of them getting on a train without me, and me alone in the big city with no one caring. All night long trains would pull in and out of the station while I stood in my Raptors jersey, crying. Crazy, eh? Here I picture myself breaking Gus's fall but getting knocked over and smashing my neck on the edge of bench. I can hear the crunch of the bone snapping and the screams of the onlookers. My spinal cord will be severed, and I'll end up in a wheelchair for the rest of my life, feeding through a tube.

And speaking of crazy, here comes old Gord. He spots me on the end of the bench. Bounces right over and stands next to me, head bent forward like always, staring down at me.

"Hiya," he says.

Gord's been around town all my life. He's greyer than he used to be, but that's the only difference. He walks everywhere, head thrust forward, smiling. He doesn't have a job, but someone must look after him. His hair is cut and his clothes are clean. When it gets cold, he wears a winter coat. Our family goes to church at Christmas and Easter, and Gord's there handing out parish bulletins, shaking hands at the door. *Hiya*, he says to everyone. *Hiya. Gord here. Wonderful to see you.* Ray always brushes past without looking at him. Mom stops to chat, using the same voice she uses for Nana. *Hel-lo. Gord. How. Are. You?* Nana's in the Golden Years Villa, slipping from tree to tree. She's maybe my favourite in the whole family. Maybe? No, she's my favourite for sure. Which makes the tree thing sadder. I'll explain that later.

"Aren't you lucky," Gord says to me now.

I stare up at him.

Lucky. That's like saying I'm tall and muscular, or Asian, or seventy-five years old. Whatever I am, I am *not* lucky.

I shake my head.

"Yes you are, you're lucky. Hiya, Lucky."

Now he's making it sound like my name is Lucky. Or my nickname. He smells of soap, I notice. Lemony. Not unpleasant but kind of strong.

"Look what I found," he says.

He reaches into his pants pocket and pulls out a disposable camera. You know the kind—black plastic, about the size of a pack of cards. You get them at dollar stores and places like Walmart. This one is wrapped in green cardboard with *SureFlash* on it.

"For you," Gord says.

"No thanks, I have a camera in my phone." I've never taken a picture, mind you.

"It's magic," he says. "A magic camera for you, Lucky."

Gord smiles at me. His teeth are grey and broken, like old tombstones.

He starts spinning. He does that, sometimes, spreads his arms out wide and spins on the spot like a, a coin on a countertop. The basketball game is going on, down at the far end of the court. No one is paying any attention to us. Gord whirls around and around, arms out wide, shirt flapping.

Oh no, I think. I don't want to be here on a park bench next to a crazy old man. I'd rather be ... I'd rather ...

And at about this moment it occurs to me that I don't know where I'd rather be. Not home, with Ray making fun of me and my parents letting him get away with it. Not in school, for sure. Not just walking around. I don't want to be anywhere, really.

Huh.

That bad weather thing inside me—that dark cloud—is part of the problem. But I won't look at it.

Gord speaks to me while he's spinning, his voice coming out of the whirlwind of baggy shirt and flailing arms.

"Twelve pictures," he says. "Twelve wishes. For you, for you, for you, for you." He breathes and spins some more. "For you, you, you, you." And again. "You, you, you, you."

That's twelve. Gord can count. But what's he getting at? What does he mean by *wishes*?

Now he stands in front of me, arms at his sides, not breathing hard despite all the spinning. Gord's in great shape. He leans forward, puts the camera in my hand. There's a little snap of electricity when we touch.

He steps back. "You're the answer, Lucky."

I want to laugh at the idea of me being the answer.

"I am?" I say. "What was the question?"

Gord points to me and then to the camera. "You," he says and backs away. "You." He keeps backing. "You!" He turns and walks off.

Weird or what? I turn to ask Lisa what she thinks, but her attention is down-court.

The *SureFlash* camera fits easily in my hand. "12 Full-Color Snapshots. Wind Aim Shoot." I put it to my eye and peer through the what-is-it, the viewfinder. I see asphalt and the toe of my running shoe. That's what I'd be taking a picture of. I check the picture indicator at the top of the camera: 0. No shots left. This camera's useless.

"Next basket wins!" calls someone from the middle of the court.

Good. When the game's over, we can go to the mall. I'm not hungry, but eating passes the time and I'll be with Magnus.

We've been friends for a long time. I got my first bike before Magnus did, and when I let him ride it, he fell off and scraped his hand and started to cry. We were about five—I guess I was *exactly* five, since I got the bike for my birthday, and Magnus would have been four and a half.

Anyway, there he was in the middle of Burnham Street, holding his hurt hand in his other one and crying hard. And wouldn't you know it, at that exact moment Ray rode up on his bike. Ray laughed, of course, because that's the kind of person he is. He called Magnus a girl for crying. The insult hurt him, I could tell. He hiccupped and blushed.

And I got mad. I told Ray to shut up, shut up, shut up. I picked up my bike with one hand and put my other arm around Magnus, even though I knew Ray would call me a girl too. Which he did. Magnus and I walked back to his place together, me pushing the bike, my arm still around his shoulders. He stopped crying after a while and thanked me for standing up to my brother, and he swore he'd never forget it—that's what he said, *I swear it*, the way kids swear things, you know?

We've been close ever since, even though Magnus got athletic and popular, and I didn't.

Nobody in Grade 8 has a girlfriend except Magnus. Lisa is the queen of the class—rich and cute and popular. She hates me. But Magnus and I are still good friends. There's a real connection between us. Some kind of—

Anyway.

Odd how easy I stood up to Ray when he was picking on Magnus. I've never been that sure of myself standing up for me.

A flurry of action, and a clang from the far end of the court. I lift the camera to my eye. There he is now in the viewfinder. His hair, his focused expression, his shoulders.

I like Magnus, but it's more than that. I think about what he might be doing and wish I could do it with him. Hanging out in his basement playing video games, jumping off the town pier into the super cold lake, eating pizza—whatever we're doing is better because he's doing it. It's like I said to Lisa—the guy's perfect. Who wouldn't want to be him?

He has total control of the ball, the game, the morning. I snap the shutter on the picture-less camera. No reason, just because. It's like I'm putting a frame around Magnus, closing the discussion.

Next thing I know I'm on my feet and everyone is shouting at me.

MAGNUS

CHAPTER 3

"To me!"

"Go! Go! Go!"

"Pass it here!"

Pass what? I wonder. Then I realize I'm holding the basketball.

How'd I get it? What am I doing on the court? *What is going on?*

I'm not much of a player. I search wildly for Magnus. He's the one who should have the ball, not me. Only I can't find him to pass to.

"To me! To *me!*" calls the shooter who missed the earlier jump shot, and a couple more in the meantime.

"Go, Magnus!" calls Haircut Gus.

He's looking right at me, but he's calling me Magnus. I don't understand ...

And then I notice other strange things about myself.

One—my cheek isn't hurting. What a relief.

Two—it's longer than usual to the ground. Which isn't as stupid as it sounds. Normally, looking down means five and a half feet or so. Now I'm farther away. Seriously, I must be over six feet tall. You'd think it would make me dizzy, but it doesn't.

Three—my arms are tanned and muscular. Which they weren't ever.

Four—there's a blue ink heart on my right bicep with *M + L* inside it.

I remember Lisa drawing that heart yesterday during math class. Not on me, though. She drew it on Magnus.

All of these new things—the height, the heart, the no zit—belong to Magnus.

Gus is yelling at me, calling me Magnus.

Which means that I *am* Magnus.

CHAPTER 4

Would you panic? I don't. I put on a big smile. I know what's going on. This isn't real. It's a fantasy. I'm getting what I wanted—to be Magnus. I don't waste any time checking my pulse or pinching myself. So I'm asleep, so what? How many chances do you get to live your dream?

The dyed blond is calling for the ball. My fake pass fools the guy guarding me. I turn and dribble down court like it's the most natural thing in the world. When big McClarty from the high school heads over to cut me off, I spin and roll past him—just like Magnus did.

I've never felt so in control of my body. For me, running has always involved a lot of flailing around, arms and legs going in different directions. Last year Miss Wideman said that when I sprinted, I looked like a building collapsing sideways.

Not in this dream, though. Not in this fantasy. I have my mind, such as it is, but I have Magnus's reflexes. As Magnus, I float down the basketball court. I see everyone. I sense a pattern of movement around me, offence and defence. I don't have to look at the ball as I dribble. I know that each bounce will bring it back to my hand.

I see Gus's haircut out of the corner of my eye. I bounce a pass to him and slip easily between two opponents. Gus gives it back to me, and I drive for the basket.

If this is a dream, it's the least dreamlike one I have ever had. The sense details are amazingly real. I can feel the seams on the basketball, hear the slightly metallic *tang* as it hits the asphalt. I can smell the sweat—theirs and mine.

The world seems normal. *I'm* the weird part, the thing that doesn't fit.

I go up for a shot, bringing two guys on the other team up with me. I make a behind-the-back pass in mid-air, which lands in the hands of my astonished dyed-blond teammate. He shoots—and misses. The rebound goes up like a mortar shot. No way I can jump high enough to grab it.

But Magnus can. I get both hands on the ball, bring it in front of me and shoot on the way down. *Swish.*

The game is over, thanks to me. We win, thanks to me. I have never ever *ever* scored the winning basket before. Or the winning goal or touchdown or run. Or anything. I don't think I have ever tiddled the winning wink before, or parred the last cheesi. You know, it's a cool feeling. These star athletes—no wonder they always seem to be smiling.

"Hey hey *hey*!" I say. "Did you guys *see* that?"

Heads turn to look at me. McClarty on the other team is frowning. Oops. Of course, it is not cool to brag. I compose my face, the way Magnus would, and accept my team's congratulations with a shrug and a smile.

"Nothing to it," I say. My voice is deep, smooth, rich. Magnus's voice.

I feel all tingly.

I wonder how long this fantasy is going to last. I keep expecting to wake up. I check the end of the park bench, figuring I must be there, dreaming away, but I'm gone—I mean, there's no one there.

Does that make sense? Not really. If I'm Magnus, then he should be me—a *Freaky Friday* thing. But he's not me. I mean, the me that was there is gone.

The world around me is correct down to the smallest detail: cracks in the pavement, cries of the lake gulls, breeze on my skin. A cloud slides over the sun, and I shiver. I can feel the change in temperature.

So real.

"Yay!" cheers Lisa. She waves, blows me a kiss. Huh. I've got a girlfriend. Who'd have thought?

Lisa's pretty, all right. Everyone says so. But I don't know. I wave half-heartedly. She squeals and comes over. And gets on tiptoe, pulls down my head, and gives me a kiss on the mouth. I've never been kissed like this before. Her lips are smooth and soft and plump. Her breath smells of cinnamon.

For you, Gord told me. Was this the gift he meant? Thanks, I guess.

CHAPTER 5

"What's that in your pocket?" Lisa asks when we break. I reach down the side of Magnus's baggy board shorts and find a small package with corners. A disposable camera. Yup, the same one—I recognize the tear in the green cardboard. I drop it back in my pocket quickly and tell Lisa it's nothing.

First thought—wow! It seems as if the camera does have some kind of magic attached to it. Just like Gord said. When I snapped the picture, I turned into Magnus. Or sort of like Magnus, 'cause I'm still me inside. My dream seems to be following its own logic.

Second thought—sooo, now what?

Should I panic? Why? I don't want to fix this. I feel kind of free. I don't have Jonah's problems anymore. No clouds overhead.

And I don't know anybody cooler than Magnus. It's fun walking around with my thigh muscles bulging and my shoulders stretching my shirt. No point in wasting time worrying about the old me. No point at all.

"What's wrong?" says Lisa.

"Uh . . ."

"Looking for Jonah? He was moping by himself on the park bench all through the game. He must have slithered off somewhere."

There's a bathtub of disdain in her voice.

"I don't know what you see in him, Magnus. I know you guys have been friends a long time, but he's such a lame-o."

"Is he?" I say. "Is he that much of a lame-o?"

"Oh, yes. And a whiner."

"Well," I say. "His brother is awful to him."

"And a slob."

"I guess he is. Those pants were the ones he wore yesterday."

"He's never happy about anything. All he does is make jokes that nobody gets."

My laugh sounds harsh. This conversation is giving me the strangest feeling. It's painful and yet satisfying too. It's like that pimple. It hurt to squeeze it, and yet I couldn't help myself.

"So why do you hang out with him?" Lisa asks. "Why do you keep telling me how funny he is, and how I should try to like him?"

And now, doofus that I am, I find myself blinking back tears. Magnus is such a good guy. Saying nice things about me.

"Well, I'm not hanging with Jonah now." I sniff.

And that's the truth. Sort of.

"Good." When she nods, her necklace bounces, catching the sunlight for a second.

I run my hand down the front of my shirt and clench my stomach. Magnus's abdominal muscles writhe like snakes. *My* abdominal muscles.

The basketball game has broken up, but a few kids are shooting at the far hoop. One of them gets pantsed as he goes up for a shot. He comes down with his shorts around his ankles and his red boxers flapping like a flag. His friends laugh. I can't help looking, glad I'm not him.

Lisa pulls my face down and kisses me again.

"What's the matter, Snoozums Woozums?" she asks.

Snoozums Woozums?

"Um," I say.

"You're looking all serious. Don't you know how lucky you are?"

"Lucky?"

"To be with me, stupid! *M* and *L*, remember?"

"Oh, right."

"And your shirt's out at the back."

"So?"

She takes me by the hand and leads me down the street. How would she feel if she knew she was holding hands with Magnus's lame-o friend—the one who tells the bad jokes? How do I feel, holding hands with a girl who despises me?

CHAPTER 6

We're in the food court at the mall, Lisa and me. She's playing with a plate of fries, and I'm finishing my last taco. She stares across the table at me.

"You're different today, Snoozums," she says.

"Huh?"

"Why did you get tacos? You don't like them."

"What are you talking about? I love them. Last week, Mag—"

I stop myself in time. I was about to say, *Magnus bet me that I couldn't eat twelve of them at one sitting, and I did,* but that would be a bad idea. As far as Lisa is concerned, I am Magnus.

"And why are you sitting on that side of the table? We always sit side by side."

"Do we? I mean, we sure do!" I move round to her side.

The movies are right—it's hard to take over someone else's identity. I look and talk exactly like Magnus, but I don't have his memories. I don't know what he knows.

But I can do what he does. I lounge back in the plastic chair, cross my legs casually, swing my ankle around. Magnus does that a lot.

Lisa is fiddling with my hair.

"There, is this okay?" She takes a small mirror from her purse, points it at me.

"Huh?" I say.

"I know how you worry about it," she says.

I do? I mean, he does?

Owen shoots at me with his finger as he goes past. He was on last year's basketball team with Magnus.

"I saw you in the park just now," he says.

"Uh, yeah," I say. "That was me."

He nods. "How'd you do?"

"Oh, you know," I say. "We won. I scored the winning basket. The usual."

"Yeah. The usual."

He smiles uncertainly. I shoot at him with my finger, and he walks away. This is kind of fun.

"Good kid, that Owen," I say to Lisa. I cross my legs the other way.

"I think he's lame-o," she says. "Almost as lame-o as— What are you *doing*?"

"Huh?"

"Licking your fingers in public. That's gross. And your shirt is out again. What's wrong with you today?"

She hands me a napkin. I use it. She's right—Magnus does not lick his fingers. And his shirts are always tucked in. It comes with being perfect, I guess. Great hair, hot girlfriend, winning basket. In fact, when I come to think of it, the part of Magnus's life that doesn't fit is me, the weird friend.

She gets this bossy look in her eyes. She stands up, grabs my hand, and pulls me through the mall, past the fitness club and travel agency and nails place. Just before we get to the elevator, she yanks me behind a fake palm tree I've never noticed before. We're in an alcove, with the mirrored outside wall of the elevator on one side and a service door on the other. We're private. No one can see us.

Lisa pulls my head down and kisses me.

Yup. Bang. Right there on the mouth.

I guess I don't react the way Magnus does. She pulls away.

"Is something wrong?" she whispers.

"Uhhh," I say.

Teachers talk about how smart I am. This is me at my smartest. *Uhhh.*

Somehow I can't get excited about someone who doesn't like me—me Jonah, I mean. Lisa would be horrified if she knew who she was smooching. I don't know why this matters to me. I enjoyed winning the basketball game, and that was fake. So why can't I enjoy a fake kiss from a hot girl? Because I don't like her either? Because kissing is more important than basketball? I don't know. But there's something.

Lisa doesn't get it either.

"Are you sick?" she asks. "Is something wrong? Is there someone else?"

"Uh, no."

"*Is there?*"

She won't believe me if I tell her the truth. I shake my

27

head. The elevator makes a dinging noise when it stops on our floor and lets people off. Lisa puts a finger to her lips. I nod and notice the head bobbing in the mirrored wall in front of me. Magnus looks a little frazzled.

"Come onnn," she murmurs. She wets her puckered lips.

We're about as close as two people can get without being inside each other's clothes, but somehow she squirms closer.

"Ouch!" she says. "Get rid of that stupid box!"

Reaching into my pocket before I can stop her, she pulls out the camera.

CHAPTER 7

"What is this?"

"Give it back," I say.

Lisa turns away to examine it.

"Why do you want this lame-o camera? You have a better one in your phone."

She isn't giving it back.

I shrug. "It's a gift," I say.

"And I didn't think you liked taking photographs, Snoozie. That's my thing. Hey, do you want to take a picture now? There's one shot left here."

"*What?*"

"See? One picture left on the counter." She shows me, but she won't hand over the camera. I move to take it back from her, but she dances away, like this is a game. "How about a picture of me?"

I'm thinking furiously. There were no pictures in the camera before. I'm sure of it. The counter read 0. Now, after I pressed the button and turned into Magnus, it reads 1. What—and I mean, *what*—is going on? If I take another picture, what'll happen to me? And will the number 1 turn into a 2?

Lisa's talking about how she's a better subject for a picture than I am, since I hate pictures of myself. "Always worried about your hair," she says.

I don't know what she's talking about. Magnus has great hair. It's a dark chestnut-y colour, with a little wave in it. I check the mirrored wall.

"My hair's fine," I say.

"That's the first time I've ever heard you say that, Snoozie. I'm glad to hear it. I'm sick of telling you how good looking you are."

"What?"

Magnus insecure? It's like finding out Hercules wets the bed.

Lisa's got her arm stretched out, pointing the camera at herself to take an old-fashioned selfie.

"Wait!" I shout. "No! Stop!"

I grab at her, try to get her finger off the button, but it's too late. The shutter comes down. And I am staring up at Magnus's shocked face.

LISA

CHAPTER 8

He staggers backwards. "What is *happening*?" he says, in a voice that sounds like mine did a second ago.

His voice, in other words. He looks around like he can't believe his senses. The elevator, the palm tree, the sound of canned mall music.

"How did I get here?" he asks. "Where's the basketball game?"

It's him, all right. Magnus. The last thing he remembers is the basketball game, before I became him. And now he's back, being himself.

He looks at me for help, guidance. Funny to see that expression on his face. Usually he's the one planning things, and I'm the one going along. That's how we are together.

"How did I get here, Lisa?" he says to me

"*Lisa?*" The name comes out of me in a high-pitched yelp, like a dog with a stepped-on tail. I've been so absorbed in staring at Magnus that I haven't realized how I've changed. I'm shorter. I'm wearing a rainbow-coloured shirt and tight (tight!) shorts. And a necklace.

And nail polish.

Oh-ho.

I check myself in the mirrored wall of the elevator. The camera took the picture, and now I am her. I am Lisa Van der Plotz, queen of Grade 8 and my best friend's girl.

"*Lisa?*" I say again. Getting used to it.

Magnus sighs and puts up his hands, smoothing his hair. "Sorry," he says in a lower voice. "Not Lisa. I meant, um, Boopie Scoopie."

"*What* did you call me?" I'm shocked, but Magnus must think I'm mad. He ducks his head.

"Boopie Scoopie." He almost whispers it.

Is he blushing? I hope he's blushing.

I don't know whether to laugh or scream. Magnus calling *me* a pet name is, well—*ridiculous* is not a strong enough word. *Boopie Scoopie?* And smoothing his hair again? This is not the friend I knew.

I'm fascinated by my reflection in the mirrored wall. Can this really be me? I push out my lipsticked lips. I flick my long dark hair. I laugh my tittery fakey tinny laugh, showing my wonderful teeth. Me.

"What's so funny?"

"Nothing, Snoozums Woozums," I say. "Nothing at all."

CHAPTER 9

It's amazing how easily we can accept total weirdness. Walking on the moon. Talking across a continent. Things that would have astonished our great-grandparents are totally normal to us. Drone attacks? Sure, we think. Internet shopping, five hundred TV channels, phone apps that make a fart sound. Lung transplants. Sour cream and jalapeño–flavoured potato chips. None of these things make sense, but we nod and say, *okay*. I guess that's what we did all those eons ago when we crawled out of the sea. What—we're breathing *air* now? Weird, but... Okay.

So today this magic camera turns me into whoever I take a picture of? Sure, I say. I am not dreaming. I am not crazy. I'm just living in a different reality.

Magnus makes a face. "What the ...?" he begins. Swallows. "I can taste *taco*. I *hate* tacos. What is going *on* with me?"

Even in this weird universe, regular rules apply. You can't be in two places at once. Magnus can't remember anything between the basketball court and the mall. I guess his, what— his soul? his self?—was asleep for all the time I was in his body. I reach up, touch the back of my hand to his forehead for a second. Mom does that to me.

"You're a little warm," I tell him. "Maybe you're coming down with something." Actually, he feels fine. His forehead is smooth and dry.

I can't get over my hands—so small and delicate.

He walks out of our little nook. Is he nervous?

"We're alone now," he says. "But you were sitting with Jonah at the park, right? Right?"

Yeah, he's nervous. Wondering how far back his confusion goes. I nod.

"I know you don't like him." Magnus sighs. "It's just . . ."

He catches sight of himself in the mirrored wall, fiddles with his hair, tucks the end of his basketball shirt into his board shorts.

"Yeah, Jonah's a smart aleck," he goes on. "And he can be a downer. But he's funny. And he can be nice too. I wish you liked him more."

He has no idea how funny that is. Or sad. Or something.

"Well, I like you," I say. Which is true.

He smiles at me. He's never smiled at me this way before. "I like you too."

CHAPTER 10

The mall music changes to a love song. Magnus's smile broadens and softens. Now it's a wide sappy grin.

"Hey, Boopie Scoopie," he whispers. "Listen. It's our special song."

He takes a step closer. I swallow.

"Two of us so much in love,
Higher than the stars above,
You're all that I'm thinking of,
Baby . . ."

I know. If I really were Lisa, I'd call the song lame-o. 'Cause that's what it is.

I've never seen Magnus so close. His eyes are the colour of syrup. And they're wet, like syrup. He puts his hands on my shoulders, leans in, and—

There's something I haven't told you.

Remember those storm clouds over my head? The dark broody weather I was afraid to look up at? I know what it is. I know what's different about me, what's going on inside. I've kind of known for a while, and that's why I've been out of sorts. It's not my brother. Yes, he's a dork, but it's nothing to do with him. It's me. And being so close to Magnus here has brought it all out in the open. The storm clouds burst. It's raining.

Can you guess where I'm going with this?

There wasn't a special moment when I knew. No light shining down from heaven, no talking poster of Lady Gaga or Neil Patrick Harris. No, there were a bunch of things. I remember watching the music video where Fernando what's-his-name was taking off his clothes and dancing around. I was, I don't know, maybe in Grade 4, just a kid, and I thought—wow. That was one.

I remember Magnus swimming in the Dresden harbour a couple of summers ago and noticing how his shoulders stuck out. Thinking he was a seriously good looking guy. I remember a dream—a bunch of dreams—that made me shake my head when I woke up.

I knew, and didn't know. I didn't want to look. I thought— no way. I'm the star of my life, and there's no way I'm gay.

Yeah, I know it's okay to be whoever you are. This isn't 1950, not even in my little town, and for all that my parents let Ray get away with too much, they're not going to disown me if I come out. Mom won't, anyway.

But it's a hill to climb. You don't believe me? Hey, you're not gay.

I've wondered about Magnus. Would the two of us ever be able to, you know, hang out? Do stuff? He's a crush, all right. He's nice and fun, and so darn good looking. I didn't come out to him, of course. I never told anyone. But I would suggest an afternoon at the beach, and at the back of my mind—the place I didn't look—there'd be a picture of Magnus without a shirt. One of the reasons I don't like Lisa is that she gets to kiss him, and I don't.

So now that I *am* Lisa and he *wants* to kiss me, it's like a free pass. Yes, I'm lying to him—he doesn't know who he's kissing. So what? I'm not proud of myself, but I'm taking the moment. And, you know, it's pretty good.

Come on, you'd do it too. Sure you would.

Funny to think about a talking poster or beam of light from heaven—a magic moment. Because that's pretty much what today is, eh?

So Magnus leans in towards me and—

Yeah.

The music drifts down like confetti.

"Two of us walk hand in hand,
On the gold and silver sand,
Of this precious fairy land,
Baby ..."

No, this is not leading anywhere. I'm not planning ahead. I'm simply enjoying the moment. And what's wrong with that? There are few enough of them in your life, after all. Savour each one.

Sure enough, this one ends with a crash.

"Your friend Jonah," I say after a minute, "may not be as bad as I thought."

Magnus's smile dazzles me. "I'm glad to hear that, Boopie Scoopie. Yeah. Jonah's a good guy at heart."

"You know," I say, "he may have a bit of a crush on you."

This is just a teaser. To see what Magnus does. He breaks away.

"What?"

Is he interested?

"Really?" he says.

"Maybe," I say, giving my hair a bit of a flip. "I've seen him look at you."

Funny to be sort of outing myself here. I'm piling a bunch of lies on each other to make a truth.

"He really likes you," I say.

Magnus shakes his head. "Nah. He can't like me that way. Not Jonah."

"Ohhh, I don't know."

"He better not! No, Jonah has problems, but not that one. He's not—" He looks around to see if anyone is watching.

My mouth is open wide. My heart pounds. No! I think. Magnus, no! Don't say it.

He says it.

"Jonah isn't a faggot," he says.

I don't stop to think. Before I know what I'm doing, I step away from Magnus, draw back my cute little running shoe and kick him. Guess where? That's right.

He gasps and doubles over.

"Faggot yourself," I say.

And I run away.

CHAPTER 11

Running is tricky when you have a purse on your shoulder and when your shorts are so tight they squeak. And when you're not in good shape, which Lisa is not. Speaking of shape, I can't help but notice that certain bits of me are, well, moving around as I run. I've never worn a bra before, so I don't know if this one is doing what it's supposed to do, but things seem very . . . how can I put it? *Precarious.* If that's the right word. I mean iffy. I feel like a Jenga tower just before it topples.

I run past shoes and books and electronics, past old ladies with canes and old men with paper cups of coffee. Past kids and moms and dads and more kids.

Magnus calls my name from way behind me.

I scurry past an empty place that will be selling jeans soon. My necklace flaps, my hair is in my eyes, and my boopies are scoopying all over the place.

Magnus yells at me to stop. I don't want to. I'm too upset. All I want to do is get away. This is beyond thinking. Or below. It is gut level.

I bump into a guy staring at a poster advertising engagement rings at Van Der Plotz Jewellers. Lisa's family's store, come to think of it. It's right up this aisle of the mall. The guy is young and hairy and smells strongly of cologne. He growls at me. I say sorry, which sounds weird in Lisa's whiny voice. She doesn't apologize very often.

I can't imagine why he's interested in engagement rings. Who'd marry him?

I run through a little boys' soccer team, knocking most of them over. Sprawled on the floor in their white and black stripes, they look like bowling pins.

"Hey, lady!" they call after me in their squeaky voices.

Lady.

I keep going. I know Magnus is right behind me. I can't face him. Can't.

On my left is a sign promising safety, though I never associated it with safety before. I race down a narrow hallway like a squirrel being chased by a basset hound, push open the first door on the left, and enter, for the first time that I can remember, a women's bathroom.

CHAPTER 12

I lock myself in a stall and sit on the lid of the toilet seat. For a moment, all I do is gasp, the sound echoing off the metal walls of the cubicle. As my heart slows down and my breathing returns to normal, I find I'm dripping on my tight shorts. Not sweat. I put my hand to my face. I didn't know I was crying.

Damn Magnus, I think. Damn damn damn.

My best friend. Used to be.

Can he still be a friend? He didn't call me a faggot to my face. Well, sort of. But he didn't know it. Is that a deal breaker? Can you be friends with a guy who says mean, stupid things about you—but doesn't *know* he's doing it?

Man, I don't want to lose him. I don't have many friends. And it's not like I was comfortable being who I was. I mean, I wasn't *out* to anybody—not even to myself—until just now. In fact, I don't even *know* that I'm out now. I don't know that I'm gay. But I might be. I probably am. And if I am gay, will I stay this way, or will I change? People do change, don't they? I used to like jelly beans and Pokemon cards. Now I don't. What if it's the same with guys?

I'm crying again. I wipe my eyes angrily.

When I *think* about maybe being gay, I'm surprised for a second, and then I think—oh yeah. Like catching sight of your new haircut. *That's* me now. Only it's bigger than that.

Magnus, you—you—you narrow-minded, mean-spirited dork. You lame-o. I'm not sorry I kicked you. I'd do it again. I don't know if we can be friends. Maybe, maybe not. But I do *not* want to talk to you now. Which brings me to my first problem—my real problem.

How to get out of here.

I don't think about being a girl. Yeah, I have body parts I'm not used to. I could get to second base all by myself if I wanted to—which I don't. And I'm really glad I don't have to pee right now. But the tricky thing is getting past Magnus. I don't want to see him, talk to him.

The mall music is piped into the bathroom. That sappy song is still playing.

Tears on my cheek. I wipe them away. Man, my skin is soft.

Someone gets into the stall next to mine. I hear a rustling and a scratchy raspy sound and some swearing. Silence. And then a whisper.

"Hey."

Is she talking to me?

"Hey, you with the flower running shoes."

That's me. Well, Lisa. The other girl is wearing red high-tops. I can see them under the partition separating the stalls.

"You got a light?" she asks.

I'm about to say I don't smoke and then realize I don't know that.

"Hang on," I say.

I feel a bit guilty taking the purse off my neck and opening it. Like I'm reading someone else's email. But I have bigger problems, and that's a nice warm voice coming from the next stall. Let's see. Lisa has a wallet and a brush and one of those snap cases of eye makeup. Also a small plastic-coated package I'm afraid to touch. I keep searching. Weird to realize that these delicate fingers with painted nails are mine.

Her phone background is a picture of Magnus in a bathing suit. I feel a rush of anger and drop the phone back into the purse. In a side pocket, I find a trove of baby Snickers bars and pop one in my mouth. Thanks, Lisa.

At the bottom of the purse, I find a plastic lighter that says *Van Der Plotz Jewellers, Dresden, Ontario*—and a disposable camera.

CHAPTER 13

I hand the lighter under the partition and take out the camera. It's the same one. The counter at the top shows the number 2. Normally, that would mean there are two pictures left in the camera. But this camera adds a number every time a picture gets taken and I turn into someone else. Twelve pictures, Gord said. *For you, for you, for you.* Whatever. I don't know what'll happen when I get to twelve pictures, but I won't be here worried about Magnus. And I won't be Lisa.

I leave my cubicle. Smoke rises in a thin blue stream from the one next door. There are No Smoking signs all over the mall. There's one right here in the bathroom. But High Tops doesn't care. She's a rebel. The sappy song is over. They're playing a peppy one that my mom sings.

So, here I am in a women's bathroom. Now what? Wait for someone to come in and take her picture, I guess. I'll become her. Then I can worry about the real me. It's the only way I can think of to get out of here and not have Magnus grab me. I put the camera on the counter and cup my hands under the tap for a drink.

There are dark smudges on my cheeks from where I was crying. They don't come off with water. I get some soap from the dispenser and lather up. The soap doesn't feel right. There's a burning sensation—like I'm holding a handful of bees. I rinse at once, and the burning goes away.

Sheesh! What would happen if I washed my face with this soap? It'd melt my skin right off me.

I hear a swear word and turn around as the stall door bursts open and a girl runs out in a cloud of smoke, frantically unbuttoning her shirt.

"Help!" she cries.

I just gape.

"Come on! Help me get this ---- thing off!"

Do I help her? Well, wouldn't you? The poor girl is on fire. Between us, we get the buttons undone and the shirt in the sink. It's a uniform. Red and white stripes. The tag on the shirt pocket says *Doreen*.

"Hi, Doreen," I say.

Five minutes ago, I wouldn't have thought I could ever smile again, but here I am with the corners of my mouth twitching up. Doreen makes me smile. She's incredibly *alive*. You know what I mean? She seems to give off a lot of energy.

She doesn't reply to me, because she's busy pouring water on the shirt and swearing. She uses one particular swear word over and over.

"---- thing caught on fire!" she cries. "---- ash from the ---- cigarette!"

I know the word, of course, but I'm not used to hearing it this frequently. I'm kind of shocked.

Doreen's a little smaller than me, the brim of her baseball cap at about my eye level. Blond hair in a ponytail under the cap, light brown skin, white bra, black jeans, red high-topped shoes. And a frown you could build a wall on.

"You okay?" I say.

She stares at me like I should explode with stupidity. "Course I'm not ---- okay!" she cries. "I've got no ---- shirt on! These ---- Cinnamon Hut shirts are the ugliest ---- things in the whole ---- universe, but at least they ---- cover you up. Now Jack'll make me buy a new one! Unless he fires me."

She's spitting like a frying pan full of bacon. Her energy is amazing. The whole room vibrates with it.

"*You* did this!" she says, pointing to the smouldering heap of polyester in the sink. "If you hadn't given me that ---- lighter I'd never have been ---- smoking in the first place. This is all your ---- fault!"

What a ridiculous thing to say. I burst out laughing. This girl is doing something to me. Shaking me up.

"---- shut up!" she says to me, but a smile twists the corner of her mouth. She knows she's being ridiculous too.

Her shirt has a small black-rimmed hole in the sleeve. She gets a handful of soap from the dispenser and rubs it on.

"Does that soap feel funny to you?" I ask.

She shakes her head, concentrating. I put the tip of my finger on the dispenser, and there's that feeling. *Bzzz.* Like the soap is hot, or poisonous.

Hmm, I think.

Of course, the soap does not get the black out. Doreen swears some more.

A lady with thick glasses comes into the bathroom, takes one look at us, turns, and leaves. I hear Magnus's voice asking her if everything is all right in here. A moment later, he calls my name.

"Lisa! What's going on? Come out!"

"No!"

I can't take a picture of Doreen and walk out as her—not without a shirt.

"Go away, Magnus!" I call.

"Who's that?" Doreen asks me.

"A—friend."

"Boyfriend?"

"It's complicated."

He pushes the door open an inch. "Lisa?" he says again. "Lisa, are you there?"

Doreen ducks behind me. "Hey! Girls only, you ----head."

I get an idea. Why didn't I think of it before? I take the camera from my purse and run to the door. I don't want to say goodbye to Doreen, because, you know, I really like her. But I don't know how to explain.

I tell Magnus to stand still a minute. Then I snap his picture through the crack in the door.

CHAPTER 14

Nothing happens. Did the camera misfire? Did I make a mistake? I press the shutter again. There's a click, but I don't find myself in the hall. I'm still in the bathroom, still Lisa. The picture counter on the camera reads 4.

I hear Gord's voice. *Twelve wishes for you.* Well, I want to become Magnus. So why can't I?

The picture counter moves, so that means the camera's not broken—which wouldn't make sense anyway, since this is some kind of magic. The magic only seems to work once per person. I can't become Magnus again.

Crap. That way out is closed. Also, I've wasted two pictures. Double crap.

"Lisa!" calls Magnus. "Come out."

"No."

I retreat into the bathroom.

"Please," he calls.

"Lisa doesn't want to come out," Doreen yells. "Go away, you ---- idiot."

The door closes softly.

Doreen holds up her shirt. The black-rimmed hole is on her sleeve, down by the cuff. It's about the size of a quarter. We stare at it.

"You're right," I say. "This is all clearly my fault."

"So help me dry the ---- thing," she says with a smile.

I push the knob on the blow dryer. She spreads her shirt in front of the nozzle. Things get hot and noisy for a few seconds, then the blower turns off. I push again.

"So you're Doreen," I say in kind of a shriek, pointing to the tag on her shirt. "Nice to meet you."

"Yeah. And you're Lisa."

"Oh. Uh, right. Yeah. Lisa."

She shakes out a cigarette, sticks it in her mouth. "You want one?"

"No, thanks."

Doreen is pretty, and she's not wearing a shirt. I get that, but I'm not feeling much.

She puffs smoke at the ceiling. "You know, Lisa, you're different than what you look like."

She has no idea how right she is.

"What d'you mean?"

"Your clothes. That purse. That necklace. You look like you'd be some snooty rich kid. But you're not. You're okay. Normal, even."

Ha. Normal. If she only knew. I push the dryer button again.

"You're okay too," I say.

And we smile at each other. A nice moment in the middle of craziness.

I ask if she has a boyfriend. She says not anymore.

"I broke up with Dave a couple days ago," she says.

"Too bad." I guess that's the right thing to say.

"S'okay. I only went out with him because he lives down the street, and he's a friend of my brother Eli's. He's a ---- jerk."

"Guys," I say. "Am I right?"

A woman bursts into the bathroom and points at us like a dog.

"Oh, there you are, Doreen! What's going on? Jack said he was going to fire you if you were late again. Oh, he is mad enough to eat hornets!"

She's older than we are, twenty-something, moist face, curly dark hair in a net. She's wearing a striped uniform shirt like the one we are drying. Her name is Elise, according to her tag. She says *oh* a couple more times while she lights a cigarette of her own.

"Burnt a ---- hole in my ---- shirt," says Doreen.

"You are in real trouble. Get dressed, and say sorry to Jack. He's so mad."

Elise takes a couple of deep drags. "Oh, I needed that!" she says, smoke wreathing her head. She notices me for the first time. "I know you," she says. "Your folks own the jewellery store."

She blows smoke right in my face.

"You complained about your cinnamini combo last week—remember? You said the buns were raw. I had to give you two fresh ones, and Jack made me pay for the whole combo. You cost me four ninety-five."

I don't know how to defend myself. Lisa could easily have done that. I remember the money in my purse. I thrust my hand in, find a five, and hand it over. Elise stares at the money suspiciously.

"Sorry," I say. "I wasn't myself that day. I'm . . . different now."

"Huh," says Elise.

"I mean it."

"Lisa's okay," says Doreen. "I like her."

Not something I hear very often.

Elise takes another drag, blowing this lungful of smoke away from me. She pockets the bill and hands me her cigarette.

"Hold onto this while I tell Jack I found Doreen. Then I can take my break."

She leaves but pops her head back in right away.

"MC!" she hisses, and disappears again.

Doreen swears, wriggling into her damp shirt.

"What?" I say.

"Mall cop."

"So?"

Doreen buttons hurriedly. "So throw away the ---- cigarette," she says, taking hers out of her mouth.

We're too late. A woman in a dark blue uniform bursts through the door and glares at us.

"Caught you again!" she says.

CHAPTER 15

The smoke alarms in this bathroom haven't worked for the last few months, and the girls from the food court smoke here. This particular cop has caught Doreen three times. She explains this to me in a low voice as we flush our smokes down the toilet. The cop yells at us. She's not real police, of course—just a bully with a badge.

"You girls are going outside," she says.

"You can't take me away in the middle of a shift," says Doreen.

"Oh, yes I can. I'll drag you if I have to, and you too, missy!"

This to me. *Missy.*

The mall cop has shoulders like an Olympic weightlifter. She could pick Doreen and me up like two parcels.

"You leave Lisa out of it," says Doreen. "That wasn't even her cigarette." A nice gesture.

The cop ignores it, steps forward with her arms out. Doreen mutters something.

"*What* did you call me?" says the cop.

Doreen is half the cop's size, but she has spirit. "I called you a ---- Nazi," she says. "Because that's what you are."

Oh, I like this girl. She inspires me. I realize that I can solve her problem, and mine, with one click of a button. The mall cop has her hand on Doreen's arm, squeezing hard. I hold up my camera.

"Hey, Nazi!" I call.

She turns with a scowl. "What did you—?"

"Say *cheese!*"

MARY LEE

CHAPTER 16

I have a headache.

My temples pound like a metal band is holding a practice inside my head. And there's something I want. I don't know what it is, but I want it a lot.

I'm looking down at Doreen. Way down. And I have a hold of her arm. I can feel my muscles squeezing her tight.

I let go at once.

"Sorry," I say.

I catch sight of myself in the bathroom mirror. Whoa. That's a tough mall cop I've turned into. I shrug my shoulders. So does the figure in the mirror. Lots of meat there. I'm kind of puffy around the face. And these eyebrows are serious.

Still in the mirror, I see Doreen staring up at me, puzzled.

"Sorry?" she says.

"Yeah. I shouldn't have grabbed you."

Doreen rubs her upper arm. "---- right," she says.

I'd smile if it wasn't for my headache.

Lisa's eyes are like soup bowls. Poor girl. Last time she

was herself, she was in the food court with her boyfriend. Now she's in the bathroom with a couple of strangers.

She screams. Course she does. She has no idea what is going on. Her mouth is so wide I can see her molars. I'd sympathize, except that my head is coming apart.

"Hey, Lisa, take it easy." Doreen puts her arm around her. "Don't let this ---- Nazi win."

Lisa leaps away from her. "Who are you?" she shrieks. "Get away from me! How do you know me?"

"What do you mean?" says Doreen. "We're friends. I know all about you. Your boyfriend's name is Magnus. You own the jewellery store here. You complained to Elise about your cinnamini combo last week. Right? Right? I know ---- everything. Come on, Lisa. You gave me your lighter. See? That's the reason we're in this ---- mess to begin with!"

Lisa stares at the lighter, opens her mouth wide to scream some more.

I am *so* tempted to walk away. My head is killing me. But there are some messed-up lives here, and part of the mess is my fault. And I find—surprise, surprise—that I care.

Mostly I care about Doreen, who makes me smile, who I really like, and who is probably wondering what the ---- is wrong with her new friend. But there's a little something inside me for Lisa too. Yeah, even for Boopie Scoopie. I can't leave her like this. Sure, she's whiny and bossy and mean. But I was her for a bit. We shared a few things. Walking away from her would be like walking away from part of myself.

She's washing her face now, patting it dry.

"What happened to me? What is going on?" she mutters.

"Wait here," I say to Doreen, and I lead Lisa outside. Magnus is sitting on the floor with his head in his hands. Is he crying?

I don't know how I feel about Magnus. Yeah, I was him for a while too, so we shared. But I'm still mad. And hurt.

He scrambles to his feet, startled, and wipes his eyes.

"Got your girlfriend here," I say. "She's a little upset. I think you two should have a long talk, okay?"

"Magnus?" She makes it a question. She's missing large chunks of time. They both are. That's got to be terrifying.

"You're short five dollars," I tell Lisa, "but you owed that to Elise at the Cinnamon Hut. Magnus here will tell you some things you did. You won't remember them, but don't worry—he deserved what happened."

Normally she'd be interrupting, but she just blinks, swallows.

"You're not going crazy," I say. "This morning will all fade away in a few days, I bet. You can go back to being your normal self."

I turn to Magnus. He's taller than I am. Tilt my head to look him in the eyes. There's something I want to say.

"You're a loyal friend," I say. "But you're stupid. I'm mad at you."

"Do I— do I know you, ma'am?" he asks.

Magnus has always been polite to grownups. My mom loves him.

"Think shorter and younger," I say. "Oh, and a guy."

"*What?*"

"Skip it."

The soccer team walks by on their way to the bathroom. One of them points at Lisa. "Hey, there she is!" They make hissing noises as they go past—six or seven boys with striped shirts and frowns. Fearless in their togetherness.

Magnus puts an arm around Lisa's shoulders. They walk away.

"Oh, Magnus," I call.

He turns.

"*Faggot*'s a bad word," I say. "It's mean, not funny. Don't use it. It'll cost you friends."

"Huh?"

"In fact, it already has."

CHAPTER 17

Back in the bathroom, Doreen is all buttoned up and tucked in. I offer to walk her to her job. She scowls up at me, asks how I know her name.

"How do I know your boss's name is Jack and that you have a mole on your shoulder?"

"Ew!" she says.

"I know a lot of things," I say.

There's something I want to do. It's making my head ache.

The food court is almost empty. Doreen and I cross slick grey tiles in silence. The smell is of hot grease and sugar and disinfectant and Chinese food and a kind of hopeless sameness. There's Elise behind the counter at the Cinnamon Hut, looking scared. Beside her is a guy with glasses and a receding hairline.

"You Jack?" I say to him. "Manager?"

He nods.

"It's about Doreen here," I say.

Elise disappears into the back. What a chicken she is.

Jack frowns. "What about Doreen?"

"Just that she's a wonderful girl!" I say. "You're lucky to have her working for you. She discovered a fire and put herself at risk extinguishing it. Do you see this?"

I take Doreen's arm, show Jack her sleeve.

"That's a burn," I say. "Your employee burned herself putting out a fire in the bathroom. That's why she's late coming back from her break."

"Oh," he says. "I thought she was wasting time."

"Nope, she's brave. I'm telling my superiors. Maybe get her a commendation."

"Really? Doreen?"

"Uh-huh."

The guy working at the sub shop next door is listening to all this. I know him—his name is Ben, and his brother Nikolai is in my class. Ben squeezes his lips into a tight bow, making a kissy face at Doreen.

"Okay then, Doreen," says Jack the manager. "I was going to fire you, but I guess I won't. Get dressed and take over here."

He goes to the back room. The hairline on his neck is straight, like a sword cut.

Doreen gives Kissy Ben the finger. Then she pops behind the counter.

"Something weird going on," she says, tying her apron. "It's like you got a brain transplant. Or you're some AI pod. I never thought I'd say this to you, but, uh, thanks."

She's closer than she knows. "Pod?" I say.

"My brother Eli reads that stuff. I don't like it. Makes me feel crazy, not knowing what's real."

"Oh, yeah." That comes out heartfelt.

Doreen asks what I'd like to drink. She won't take any money.

"On the ---- house," she says. "You did me a favour. Jack was looking for an excuse to fire me. Lucky you caught me smoking."

I raise my paper cup of Dr Pepper.

"That's me," I say. "Lucky."

A guy in a buzz cut strides up to the counter and orders cinnamon buns for himself and his boy. "Lots of icing," he says. "Last time there wasn't enough. Right, Greg?"

Greg's the kid I saw on his driveway earlier—the one in the Red Wings sweater. He nods cautiously. His eyes are on a level with the counter. Dad seems like a jerk, but I can't save Doreen from everyone. I have my own problems. I finish my Dr Pepper and say goodbye. She waves. She doesn't know my name. Well, neither do I.

CHAPTER 18

My mall ID card, clipped to my dark blue button-down shirt, provides the answer to who I am. I examine it as I walk away from the food court.

I'm Mary Lee Marzan. I'm five foot nine inches tall, I have brown eyes, and I am homely. Official photos make everyone look bad (you should see my class picture from last year), but this one makes Mary Lee look like a toad-woman.

I find more info about me in my pockets. I can drive. I'm—I have to work it out—thirty-three years old. I belong to a gym. And I quit smoking, because there's a pack of gum that's supposed to take away the cravings. Which explains my headaches, and maybe why Mary Lee was so tough on the smokers in the first place.

I pop a piece of gum in my mouth. I hope it'll make me feel better.

My blue uniform pants have deep pockets. I walk through the mall with my hands in them. The walkie-talkie on my belt crackles urgently. I can hear words through the static. Something about a Code 5. I'm probably supposed to respond with *10-4* or *Roger* or something. I press the send button.

"Hi," I say.

"Mary Lee? Didn't you hear? Code 5 in sector C-1! Over."

"Okay," I say. Mary Lee has to take some Code 5 action—grab a scrunchie shoplifter in Ardene maybe. I don't care. I go back to walking and thinking, my right hand clutching the camera in my hip pocket.

An old lady sits on a display chair in front of the furniture store. I get a sudden memory of Nana—wispy hair, wet eyes, and a dress with buttons down the front. This lady's dress is dirty, though, and her shoes are cracked. She starts when she sees me.

"Please, miss, I just got here," she says. "Just a few minutes ago. Please don't ask me to move again. I'm so tired."

Her bundle buggy rests beside her. Her fingers twist in her lap like small shy sea creatures waving on the ocean bed.

I walk on quickly. I'm ashamed. What kind of person would ask this old lady to move? Doreen was right. I'm a ---- Nazi. Geez, Mary Lee, get a life.

The stores are practically empty. Clerks stand outside, calling across to each other. *Did you hear?* they say, and *Isn't it strange?* and *Are the police there yet?*

And then, totally out of the blue—well, this is inside the mall, so totally out of the light greeny grey—here comes Gord. He hurries straight towards me, head forward, shirt flapping, hand out for me to shake.

"Hiya, Lucky," he says. "Wonderful to see you again."

We're in front of the pet store. Tropical fish in the window next to us. Colourful and shimmery, like rainbows flowing down the glass walls of the store.

"You know me," I say.

"Sure. Sure. You're Lucky," he says. "From the park this morning. I gave you something."

I bring my hand out of my pocket.

"Yeah, yeah, that camera. It's for you, eh? How are you liking it?"

"You recognized me, even though I look different. So you know what the camera does."

He blinks. "It takes pictures."

"It's magic!" I say. "You know that. You saw through me. I'm not Jonah anymore. I'm Mary Lee."

My first thought is relief. Overwhelming relief. Someone else knows what is going on. I'm not alone. I'm not crazy.

I grab Gord's arm.

"Why?" I ask. "Why did you give this to me?"

I'm gripping pretty tight, but he has no problem pulling free.

"Am I supposed to change?" I ask. "Is that it? Am I supposed to become someone else?"

I guess I'm yelling. I'm angry—or scared—or maybe I'm scared underneath angry. Gord doesn't react, though. He has his usual smile.

"Change is good," he says.

He points to the top of the camera. The dark parts of his eyes are flecked with gold. "You've used five chances," he says. "See? 5."

71

I've been three different people. The other two pictures must be the ones I took of Magnus—where the camera clicked but nothing happened.

"So I've got seven pictures left. Seven chances to change who I am."

"The camera doesn't really change you," he says.

"What do you mean? Look at me. I'm an ugly mall cop. I'm different."

"You're Lucky." The broken-toothed smile is sweet and sad. "That's who you are." He hurries away, head bobbing, shirt billowing.

In the pet store window, the tropical fish are playing follow-the-leader.

"Wait! Gord! Where's my body?" I go after him. "Where's the real me?"

He disappears into a crowd of people and around a corner. The corridor is totally jammed. Reminds me of Malloween or Boxing Day. I edge forward, looking for Gord, not finding him. I end up at the front of the crowd. Police are keeping us back. The cop nearest me nods, like he knows me.

"What's going on?" I ask him.

"Didn't you get the Code 5, Mary Lee?"

Van Der Plotz Jewellers—Lisa's family store—is beside the main entrance to the mall. Gold lettering on the sign, display cabinets filled with crystal swans and stuff like that. No prices in the window, no slogans, no sales. Not like the store next to it, where Uncle Al sells Mennonite furniture, and everything is always 75 percent off.

A typical Van Der Plotz saleswoman stands in front of the store now. She has one of those fake tans that's more orange than brown, so that her round, rough-skinned face looks like a Ritz cracker. She's wearing earrings and rings and a sparkly pin thing on her jacket. Like I say, it's no surprise to find her in front of a jewellery store. The surprise comes from the guy with her. He's standing behind her, so we can't see his face. He's got one arm around her neck, choking her. And he's holding a knife against her cheek.

This Code 5 is a *hostage* incident?

Police guard the entrance, keeping customers out. There's an open area between the crowd in the corridor and the hostage. Standing there, all by himself, is a guy in a base-ball jacket. He has to be a cop too. Senior, if he's in plain clothes. He seems to be the negotiator. He speaks slowly, calmly. Loud enough for everyone to hear.

"Put the weapon down, son," he says, taking a slow step forward. "You don't want to make this worse than it is."

"Don't come any closer!" yells the guy with the knife.

The negotiator stops moving. "Sure," he says. "No problem."

He's about my dad's age, looks like he has kids and a mortgage and sore feet.

"What's your name, son?" he asks. "No reason why we can't be friendly. I'm Inspector Chomitz. What do they call you?"

"My name is Phil." Deepish voice with a quiver in it.

The crowd around me goes *Ahhh*. It's a better story when there's a name. We're acting like this is some kind of free show. A whole lot of cell phones are in the air, shooting pictures and movies. The guy beside me takes out a pack of Juicy Fruit gum and pops a piece in his mouth without taking his eyes off the scene. It's as if he's at home watching TV.

"Nice to meet you, Phil. How old are you?"

"Seventeen."

"Fantastic!" says the inspector. "If you were a year older, this situation could get rough, Phil. You'd be tried as an adult and go to jail. But you're still just a kid. If you put down the knife now, on your own, you can pretty much walk away."

"I don't want to walk away," says Phil. "I want her to say sorry!"

The inspector nods, looking sympathetic, wanting to understand.

"*Who* do you want to say sorry?"

"Her!" Phil shakes his hostage. "Old lady Van der Plotz here. She was rude to me. I wanted to buy a ring for my girl, and she wouldn't let me. Said I had to leave the store. She was rude!" He looks at her. "You're a rude old woman!"

He leans forward, so we see his face for the first time. Hey—it's the guy I bumped into when I was running away from Magnus. The growling guy who was staring at engagement rings.

CHAPTER 19

'm not surprised. You know how the police find some guy with a dozen bodies buried in the backyard, and all his neighbours are shocked? Not Phil's neighbours. They're going to say, *Oh, that guy! I always thought he was a creep.*

"Don't hurt her, Phil!" The inspector's voice has an edge in it. "Let's work together. Come on, son. Don't look at her. At me. Okay? Good. Now, you're not happy, are you? We wouldn't be here if you were happy. So, what do you want?"

His voice echoes around the hard edges of the mall, the glass storefronts, and the tiled flooring. *What do you want?*

"I want her to say sorry."

Phil's arm tenses around the old lady's throat. He's pretty well built, got a good set of biceps that pop out of his short-sleeved shirt. I can make out a tattoo of some kind—an animal—on his forearm.

"Okay, that's easy," says the inspector. What's his name again? Chomitz. "Relax and let the lady apologize. How about it, ma'am? Can you say you're sorry? Phil, take your hand away. The lady will talk, you'll feel better, and we can all go home. I don't know about you"—his voice lightens— "but I missed lunch, and I'm hungry."

The crowd goes *Ahhh* again.

Reluctantly, Phil loosens his hold. Enough to let the woman say something. And she does. She opens her mouth and speaks with the dry cold crunch of a winter day.

"You are a piece of *trash*!"

Phil tenses like a spring. "What did you say?"

"Trash!" She has a voice that carries. "That's what you are. What my granddaughter calls a lame-o. You can't afford a five-thousand-dollar ring. You were going to steal it, weren't you? I didn't trust you, and I was right. Trash like you *belongs* in jail!"

"That's it!" Phil tightens his grip so that Mrs. Van der Plotz is right up against him, and he brings his knife up, the point touching her neck. The cops do that *click click click* thing with their pistols, bringing them up to fire.

The old lady's still talking. "Are your parents trash too? Probably. Probably your whole family is trash."

"Shut up!" he shrieks. "Shut up, you old bag! I hate you!"

Inspector Chomitz has his hands down at his sides. He's out of ideas. Who can save the situation now?

"You, Lucky," says a voice near my ear.

I turn my head, and there's Gord. Where'd he come from? A second ago, I was standing next to Juicy Fruit guy.

"You are the answer," he says. "*You* help."

I stare at Gord, like, *Me*?

He nods.

The crowd gasps some more. Phil flexes his left arm—the one around the old lady's neck. The knife in his other hand is shaking.

"Why?" I ask. Meaning, *why me?* Why am I the answer? I don't know why *Gord* can't be the answer, since he knows so much. Also, why should I do anything to help *Mrs. Van der Plotz*? I don't like her.

"Do it for you," he says. It's like he can read my mind.

Okay, I don't like her, but I guess I don't want her to get stabbed. And if the question is *Who can take a picture and change this scene?*—I am the answer. I reach for the camera.

I could become her and apologize, and then Phil would probably let me go. Probably. But maybe not. He is a weirdo, after all. And if he stabbed anyway, he'd be stabbing me. These thoughts flash through my mind.

Speaking of flashes, I can see lights on top of police cars through the glass doors of the mall.

The sky is grey. The perfect morning has turned threatening.

As I lift the camera to my eye, I hear a roll of thunder.

PHIL

CHAPTER 20

'm getting used to the way it works. Entering someone else's body is like waking from a deep sleep. A strong sense of *Where am I? How did I get here?*

There are gasps and moans from the crowd, but I'm getting a weird thrill. An *oh yeah!* feeling. Thing is, I'm not feeling sympathetic to Mrs. Van der Plotz. Yeah, she's my hostage, but she's also snooty and mean. And she reminds me of Lisa—and Ray. And now she's going to get stabbed. That's kind of thrilling. Creepy and terrible, but thrilling.

A great weight has been lifted from me. I don't have a constant headache. That's a relief. And I'm a guy again. Being a girl isn't a weight, but it's different. Like watching a British TV show, where the cars come at you from the wrong side of the road.

Otherwise, I'm not doing so good. I don't want to be holding a knife against Mrs. Van der Plotz's wrinkled neck. On top of everything else, she smells bad. Perfume, sweat, fear, body odour. No, wait, some of that is me.

I drop my knife hand to my side and apologize. "Sorry," I say. "Really sorry."

Mrs. Van der Plotz calls me lame-o again. Odd to hear Lisa's favourite word come out of her old mouth, but she's got a point. Phil *is* lame-o. In a louder voice, I say I'm having second thoughts. The crowd sighs. The inspector tells me that's great. He's got a big smile for me, nods in approval.

"Now, let Mrs. Van der Plotz go, okay, Phil?"

There are cops everywhere, and they're all pointing guns at me. I feel like a specimen on a slide. The rain is beating on the glass doors of the mall.

"And I can walk away from this?" I say.

"Oh, yeah," Inspector Chomitz says, with an understanding smile. "You're a mixed-up kid, Phil. We'll have lots of sympathy for you."

"I don't want to hurt this lady."

"That's good, Phil. Real good. Now, about the knife. Can you drop it?"

It's some kind of flick knife—black plastic handle, longish straight blade—but I can't close it. In the movies they just shake their wrist and the blade vanishes, but this one doesn't.

"Sorry," I say.

"Just drop it, Phil. Drop it on the floor. Come on, buddy."

I open my hand, and the knife clatters to the floor by my foot. The crowd goes *Oooh*. The inspector asks me to kick the knife away from me. I do. And the crowd *oooh*s again, even longer this time. And then is silent.

"I'm proud of you, son," he calls.

"D'you mean it?"

I try to think of the last time I heard my dad say he was proud of me.

"I mean it. You're doing the right thing." He wipes his forehead. "We're almost finished now," he says. "All you have to do is let go of the lady."

"Oh, right," I say.

I've been holding on to her this whole time. Didn't notice, because I was paying attention to the knife and the crowd and the cops, but my left arm is still clamped around her soft, bony shoulder.

"Step away from her, and let her walk towards me. Can you do that, Phil?"

I say yes.

"Good stuff, buddy."

I drop my hand and step away, and Mrs. Van der Plotz totters forward on her high heels. Two cops run to grab her. The crowd applauds, which makes me feel better than I have in a while. Take that, Ray. When was the last time *you* saved a life?

Wow. I feel almost comfortable. Dozens of people are taking my picture. Cell phones, mostly, but the local newspapers are here too. I recognize the tall woman with the short haircut. Peg something. She's taken Ray's picture before.

Which reminds me that I should get out of here. The camera is in Phil's right front pocket. I've been aware of its sharp edges poking into my thigh all along. I scan the crowd for an isolated figure, someone I can take a picture of. I want to make an unobtrusive body switch.

83

Tight jeans Phil wears. I can't get my hand in the pocket right away—

"He's got another weapon!"

I look round. Three police officers are in firing stance—legs apart, two hands on the pistol, pointing at me. Shrieks from the crowd. Flashes. Movement. Everyone trying to get out of the way.

"Hands!" shouts the inspector. No smile at all. "Keep your hands where we can see them, Phil!"

He has his own pistol out.

"But I just want—"

"In the air! Both of them! Now!" He's shouting.

I do it. He tells me to lie on the floor and put my hands on my head or he'll shoot me. He sounds less understanding than he did just a minute ago.

I get down on the floor, first on my knees and then on my stomach. Two cops jump on top of me and grab my wrists.

"Ow, careful," I say.

They ignore me, almost pull my arms out of the sockets getting me into handcuffs.

"I'm just a mixed-up kid," I say.

The camera's in my front pocket, but it might as well be in Peru.

Blur time. Cops empty my pockets and hustle me out of the mall. I catch a glimpse of Mary Lee at the front of the crowd, choking. I guess she was surprised to be chewing her anti-smoking gum. Poor mall Nazi. But I have my own worries.

It's raining. A woman pops out from under an umbrella and points a microphone at me.

"Why'd you do it?" she yells as they push me roughly into a police car.

Good question. She means, why did I hold the lady hostage? But I'm thinking, why did I listen to Gord?

The back of the police car smells of disinfectant. The windows don't roll down. I lean forward to take the weight off my cuffed hands, which are hurting. The car accelerates, throwing me back against the seat.

One thing I've learned: no matter how bad things are, they can always get worse. Always.

I'm astounded at how badly things have gone—and how fast! I was happy as Magnus, winning the ball game. That was, what, a couple of hours ago? Since then, I've lost my friend, my freedom, and my chance to escape.

I'm a failed small-town terrorist, and my magic camera is gone.

CHAPTER 21

'm in an interview room at police headquarters, unable to answer any questions. I don't even know my full name. The police sergeant has to get it from my wallet. She thinks I'm uncooperative. I'm not, I'm just ignorant.

The room is small, windowless, with two chairs and a table. My interview is being taped on an old portable machine. For the record, I'm Philip Edward Abrams. I'm seventeen, and I live on Spring Street in Hope Springs, one town over from Dresden.

The sergeant's name is Brown. The other cops call her Virginia. She wants to know about my knife and my girlfriend. When I can't tell her, her lips tighten. She doesn't yell or anything, but I can tell she's angry.

That inspector at the mall is a liar. Police have no sympathy for mixed-up kids. None. They hate me here. They led me through the squad room on my way in. An officer with a big moustache glared at me like he wanted to roast and eat me and spit out my bones.

Things look pretty grim.

No, make that *really* grim.

There is no escape. The camera is in a clear plastic bag on Sergeant Brown's desk, and I won't get it back until I'm out of prison, which, she says, could be years. Years! I'm Phil for the foreseeable future. Inside the camera there are, what, six chances to be someone else, but I can't get to them. It's scary.

Why did I take a picture of Phil? With Gord talking in my ear, it seemed like the right thing to do, like he had a plan for me. How can being here be part of his plan? And what kind of idiot does it make me, to think this?

The table in front of me is heavy, ugly, indestructible. Old burn marks on the top. Virginia asks me how things are at home.

"You and your parents get along?"

I don't know what to say. I'm freaking out here.

"I remember being seventeen," she says. "My old man didn't understand why I wanted to be a cop. We'd stand in the middle of the living room, yelling at each other. Mom stayed in the kitchen, wringing her hands. Your dad yell at you?"

I shake my head. Dad sighs a lot. I wonder how he'd react to me being in jail? About the same as to me being gay, I bet. He'd sigh. Mom would smile cheerfully and talk about her next prison visit. But she'd be wringing her hands inside.

The tape recorder hisses for a while. In my mind, I connect the burn marks to make different patterns in the tabletop—a star, a house, a crab. Virginia asks more questions I can't answer. She's polite, but I can tell she thinks I'm awful. After a while, it gets to me.

"Look!" I finally say. I lean over the table with my hands out. "I agree with you. I think Phil's a creep too. I don't like him. I don't want to be him."

As I'm speaking, I hear the echo of my words. Are they true? Of course I don't want to be Phil. But then, do I want to be me?

You're lucky, Gord had said. Yeah, right.

"Do you understand what you're saying?" asks Virginia.

"Better than you do. But there's nothing I can do about it now."

The interview's over. Virginia takes me to a cell in the back corner of the squad room. The bars rattle when the door clangs shut.

There's two of us in jail back here—two small cells, separated by a common wall of bars. My neighbour's asleep with the covers up over his head.

I lie down on the cot and count my blessings. That doesn't take long.

I can't see all of my tattoo because it's around my upper arm. Some kind of dragon, I think. Phil is in good enough shape that the tattoo works for him. He's not a bad looking guy. Too bad he's such a weirdo. What was he thinking? I bet he wasn't thinking anything. I bet he got to the store, and Mrs. Van der Plotz was a jerk to him, and he reached for his knife. Events got out of hand. They do, sometimes. She was mean, and Phil was angry, and, well, a cow flew by.

That's Magnus's phrase for when he does something crazy, when his brain shuts down for a second. He'll make a terrible move, and the zombies will get him, and his reason will be, *A cow flew by.* Maybe that's why Phil took the old lady hostage, and why I snapped his picture. There seems to be a whole flock of cows out there today.

Magnus.

Still hurts, hearing that word, *faggot*, in his voice. It's way harder to think about Magnus than to think about being myself. Friends matter.

I lie back and work on my breathing. When there's nothing you can do, do nothing. I close my eyes and go inside. I'm on a subway train that's rushing like mad through a tunnel. We pull into a station with no sign. Magnus is waiting there. The train rolls right through the station without slowing down. Next station, there's Doreen. The train rolls through. I'm getting worried. I don't want to miss my stop, but I don't know which one is mine. We emerge from underground. Now we're racing across the prairie. We're getting farther and farther from my stop. I force open the doors and jump. The train races past in a series of clanks and puffs. I get to my feet. I'm me. I can feel the new pimple on my cheek. The prairie stretches away in all directions. I'm alone. I hear the *clank clank clank* of the train receding in the distance.

I wake up. The *clank* is my cell door opening. I sit up with a start. Virginia the sergeant tosses me a paper bag from Tim Hortons. I thank her.

"Your parents just left," she says.

"*My* parents? Oh, you mean ... them. Right," I say.

I was asleep and forgot who I am. *My* parents were one of my few blessings. They let me make a phone call. I left a message on the answering machine at home to say that Magnus had invited me to his house for a while. Now Mom won't worry.

The sergeant is talking about Phil's parents.

"They didn't want to see you," she says. "And they aren't doing anything about bail or a lawyer. We have arranged for legal aid, but I don't know when your lawyer can get here. If you were hoping to go home soon, forget it."

I think about parents and kids. Home life is a mystery. You can know someone really well and have no idea what goes on in their family.

"Leon!" calls the sergeant, opening the door to the other cell next to mine. "Leon!"

I pop the top on my can of root beer. Phil has muscles. They bulge under his clothes like tennis balls. He clearly spends time in the weight room with the other guys.

"Leon! Wake up!"

There's a stirring beneath the blankets next door, and a tousled head appears.

"Soft you now, the fair Ophelia," he says. "Nymph, in thy orisons be all my sins remembered."

"Sure," says Virginia. "You hungry? Your release papers haven't come through yet, so you get a snack too."

She tosses him a bag like mine. He sits up, yawning.

"O appetite, from judgment stand aloof," he says. "Food is the summons that brings us all to the highest court."

He's got an English accent. *Court* sounds like *coat*. He could go to one of those snooty schools, Hogwarts or someplace.

His face is small, elfin. Or maybe it just looks that way

inside all his hair. I realize that the word *tousled* doesn't do his head justice. He's got a gigantic mess up there. An explosion, a hurricane of hair.

"And what have you selected for my delectation this fine afternoon, O Virgin Queen?" he says. "Foie gras with truffles? Quails' eggs? Larks' tongues?"

"Maple doughnut," she replies with a smile. I can tell she gets a kick out of this guy. "And a drink."

He opens the bag, sniffs deeply. "Hello, transfat, my old friend," he says. "I've come to talk with you again."

He notices me. "Another young guest at your hostelry, fair Ophelia!" he says, with a nod towards me. "A companion in misfortune. How wonderful and sad."

"Phil here is sad all right. But I don't know about wonderful."

She walks away. Leon smiles at me through the bars. He doesn't seem too concerned about what the sergeant said about me.

"Ophelia has performed our introductions for us," he says. "Thereby obviating the necessity for self-advertisement. Is that not lucky?"

"Lucky?" It's about the only word he's said that I understand.

"Well, yes. Propitious. Advantageous. Opportune. Fortuitous."

"You're calling me Lucky?"

"Well, aren't you?" he says. "It is surely a question of perspective. You've a place to lie down, no decisions to make, and a free snack. Yes, you're lucky all right."

We eat on our cots, cross-legged. The squad room is right outside our cell doors, but the police officers ignore us. Leon is dressed like a kaleidoscope, in a long loose coat patched with bits and pieces of striped and patterned cloth. His hair is an angry mob, dashing off in all directions.

"You aren't the only person to call me Lucky today," I say. "The name seems to be following me around. Even though it's not my real name."

"Shall I call you Phil, then? Thou hast thy Phil of blood and death! Phil all thy bones with aches! Ha!"

"Phil's not my name either."

"Now I'm getting confused," he says. "The wind must be north–northwest."

There's something about food. I'm buried in trouble, feeling so low that I'd kiss my brother in exchange for getting out of here. (Would I really? Well, maybe.) I am trying desperately not to think ahead, not to look at the sergeant's desk. And yet as I eat, I find myself feeling better. Is it the snack? Maybe it helps to have Leon nearby. He's in trouble too, and he's not worried. He smiles at me like a . . . well, like a friend.

"You know, this is an awesome doughnut!" I say with my mouth full.

Leon nods. "Hunger is the best sauce. And there is something about quiet that conduces to digestion. Better the beans and bacon of peace than the cakes and ale of fear."

Leon has his sleeves rolled up to eat. I notice some writing on his pale hairless forearm—big sprawly letters in pen. *I SAVE*. I sometimes write on my arm to remind me to do something. *Dentist*, I will write. Or *Grandma birthday present. I SAVE* makes me think of one of those hoarders on TV. Or a banker. Or a goaltender.

Sergeant Brown comes over, holding her cell phone.

"Hey, Leon, I just got a message from Martha," she says. "The mayor's not going to prosecute. She's on her way over here now with the release papers. You'll be home in an hour."

"You become yourself, most beautified Ophelia!" he says, licking icing off his fingers. "You are a model of a modern policeman, though your lot be not a happy one." His face changes. "That is an ill phrase, do you not think? A vile phrase."

She laughs. "What, a policeman's *lot*?"

"No, *beautified. Beautified* is a vile phrase."

She walks back to her desk, shaking her head.

"Why did you say the wind must be from the north-northwest?" I ask Leon.

His smile is amazingly sweet. "When it's from the south, I can tell a hawk from a hand grenade."

While we're waiting for his release papers, we talk. He's full of stories, Leon is, and he makes a big production out of telling them. His eyes get wide and excited, and he shuffles up and down, waving his arms. I feel almost calm, next to him. The wilder his stories, the less I panic.

He uses lots of words I've never heard before, but they seem to make a kind of sense coming from his mouth. Some of the stories are creepy, about witches who tell the future, and monsters and spirits who come when you call. But some of them are really funny. There's one about a queen who falls in love with a donkey—it makes me laugh out loud. There's another one about a forest that walks across Scotland. I tell him he has to be kidding, but he assures me that it's all written down.

"Sure 'tis passing strange, but then the world is full of such things, do you not agree—you who are neither Phil nor Lucky?"

I agree, all right.

"What's the strangest thing that has ever befallen you?" he asks quietly.

I'm still thinking of the wood marching across the countryside, getting in people's way. (Can you imagine? You're playing road hockey and someone shouts, *Tree-ee!* and you all have to stand aside while this forest goes by.)

"What's the strangest thing that ever happened to me?" I say. "That's easy. Because it's happening right now."

My turn for a story, and, stranger than strange, I find myself telling Leon about my day. The whole thing, from the basketball game on. I don't worry about whether he'll believe me. My story is no stranger than some of his.

I tell him everything. Yup, even the kissing. I get going on my story, and then I just keep going. I'm as far down as I can get. I don't care anymore. Also, Leon's so weird, so outside normal, that I actually care what he thinks. I mean, I'm no weirder than he is.

He leans forward, listening intently. When I'm done, he says it's wondrous pitiful. He says he's never heard a tale so confused, so strange, so outrageous, and so variable. And other stuff like that.

"And it all started with the camera Gord gave you," he says.

"Yup. That one." I point through the bars into the squad room. Sergeant Brown's desk is the nearest one to us, and the plastic bag with my belongings is sitting right there. So near. So unreachable.

Leon's accent makes *Gord* come out sounding a lot like *God*. Funny, eh? Gord in heaven. Gord have mercy. Gord almighty.

"So you are not the criminal they think you are," he says. "A miscarriage of justice! Unlucky Lucky! Oft our displeasures, to ourselves unjust, destroy our friends and after weep their dust."

His cheeks are dotted with freckles, like candy sprinkles. His chin has a teeny dimple.

"Whatever," I say.

CHAPTER 22

There's a rumble of thunder outside. The day is staying nasty.

"How do you remember the other people?" Leon says. "How can you find your way to all those homes?" His voice drops. "I have only one home, Lucky, and yet I keep getting lost."

"I don't even know where home is," I say.

The lights flicker for an instant, and thunder makes the windows in the police station rattle. Leon shuffles towards me, with his hair following, and reaches through the bars. His hand feels warm on my arm.

"You should seek out the giver of the gift," he says. "You should find Gord."

"I guess," I say.

I was happy to see Gord in the mall—but look what happened. I'm here in jail because of him. *You* help, he said. And I helped, and now look at me.

"I'll direct thee how thou shalt escape," says Leon. "Then come thou to me and see him."

What is he saying? "See who?"

"Gord."

"Do you know the guy I mean?"

Leon nods. He's got small dark eyes, like raisins.

"Gord lives with me," he says calmly. "He does some work around the place. His room is upstairs. He comes and goes."

What? I mean, *what*? Talk about coincidence.

"Really?" I say.

"He was there when I moved in, and he's still there, like Mama and Martha and the Board of Health. He helps in the garden. A secret and enterprising man."

Board of Health? What kind of home life does Leon have?

"This is where I live," he says, holding out his arm. "I show this to people when I'm lost. Martha told me to write it somewhere I would not forget."

I SAVE.

And just as I am about to tell him that that makes no sense, Sergeant Brown comes over, dangling her keys.

"Martha's here to take you back to 5th Avenue, Leon."

"It's a wise child that knows his own bedroom," he says.

The sergeant laughs. "That's because you sleep in other people's."

And now I get it.

"So you live at number 1, 5th Avenue?" I say. *I SAVE* is really *1 5 AVE*. That's what Leon shows to people when he is lost.

He grins. Something happens inside me. Or maybe something is already happening inside, and Leon speeds it up. I know what I have to do. I was freaked out, and he calmed me down. Now he's giving me something to look forward to. It's like I'm on a thrill ride.

"It's a group home," the sergeant explains. "Sort of a half-way house. You might end up there yourself, Phil. Just don't count on this guy to find the place—eh, Leon?"

She's not as down on me now that Leon and I are getting along.

"I am always getting lost," he says.

"This morning the mayor came out of the shower and found him in her bed, snoring away. She got mad and called us. What were you thinking, Leon?"

"Full fathom five her bedroom lies," he says. "Her sheets are coral. And they have cracker crumbs in them."

"Really," says the sergeant. "Crumbs in the mayor's bed?"

"Well, they're there now."

Leon puts his hand through the bars we share. I take it.

"Come visit me. And Gord?" he says. "In whatever guise you find yourself."

"I'll do that. If I ever get out of here."

"And thanks for your story, Lucky. All of it."

His eyes hold me. I didn't actually come out to him. But I practically did. Is that what he means? Is *he* maybe . . .? Wow. He's a weirdo, but he's pretty cool. Amazingly cool. That thing inside me happens again.

"Stay and be secret," he says. "Myself will go. Have no fear. Journeys end in—well, you know where journeys end."

"Huh?" I say.

"It's a phrase. That's all. Have faith and doubt not of a fair and Lucky war."

As usual I don't understand him, but that's okay. Hope bubbles up inside me, bright, warm, unstoppable.

Sergeant Brown leads Leon to her desk. A frown-and-glasses lady is waiting for him. A *caring* lady. Her face is wrinkled and tough, like an old apple. He calls her Martha. She tries to smile, gives up. She looks like she spends her whole life walking into the wind.

Leon's colourful coat shimmers as he bends over the desk to sign something. He straightens up, holding the plastic bag of my belongings at his side. No one's paying attention to him. He catches my eye and grins at me again—the full-face lively grin that makes my heart pound. In a smooth clean motion, he tosses the bag in my direction. I see it in the air, turning end over end. I reach my hands through the bars to catch it, fumble open the Ziploc, and pull out the camera. The bag drops to the floor of my cell.

This is my chance. My pot of hope bubbles over. I know what to do. What an amazing ten minutes this has been. Thank you, Leon. Thank you.

Sergeant Brown lets out a yell and heads towards me. So does a bulky cop with a mouthful of chewing gum. So does a small cop with a mean expression and a nightstick in his hand.

Three of them and one of me. I back myself into the cell, point the camera blindly at the far end of the police station, and click the shutter.

MR. ELEGROOTER

CHAPTER 23

"Hang on a second, gentlemen. There's something going on in the cells."

The officer with the big black moustache—the one who wanted to chew me up and spit me out when I was Phil—peers across the squad room.

"Everything all right over there, Virginia?" he calls.

"Yeah, Darren." Sergeant Brown's voice comes from somewhere behind me. "Nothing serious. We got it covered."

I'm not Phil anymore. I am sitting in a visitor's chair in the squad room. I cannot tell you how happy I am.

Moustache Darren apologizes for the disturbance. "It's a punk kid acting up," he says. "I hate them."

Leon's on his way out the front door behind Martha. He checks around the squad room. He knows I'm somewhere in here. I try to wave to him, but I can't—and then he's gone.

What a guy he is—a wonderful crazy guy. I want to adopt a bunch of pets and call them all Leon. All of them. *Come and get it, Leons!* I'll call at feeding time, and the dogs and cats and ferrets and hamsters and iguana will come running.

But wait—something's wrong. My arm hurts. That's why I can't wave. What's going on?

I sit next to a window. Raindrops trace narrow trails of hope down the dirty glass. My arm isn't the only thing that hurts. So does my neck and back and hip. My whole body hurts. The pain isn't in the background. It's constant, threatening, a mosquito whining through my life.

"Where were we, gentlemen?" asks Darren.

I have no idea. The guy beside me does, though.

"I'll tell you where we were," he says, in a voice from the bottom of his boots. "We were at the part where Elegrooter here spit on my wife's grave!"

He glares at me. Eyebrows like winged birds.

"What?" I say.

Am I Mr. Elegrooter, from around the corner? Old Elegrooter, who has lived in the neighbourhood forever? Yikes. Don't get me wrong—I'm not in jail and that's fantastic. But—Elegrooter?

"You heard me, you skunk! You know how much Gwennie cared about Patches! When you ran over him with your show-off new toy, you were spitting on her grave."

I know this guy too—he's Elegrooter's neighbour, another really old man. He must be talking about the rider mower, the one I saw being delivered this morning.

"Patches?" I say.

I try to get up. Can't. My back gives a twinge. Of course, I'm wearing a windbreaker. Everyone my age wears one.

When I sway forward, I feel the weight of a familiar package in the right hand pocket. That's a relief.

Thunderclap. The window rattles.

I can't think of the neighbour guy's name. He looks like a mean Pillsbury Doughboy. He lifts a paper shopping bag off the floor. Whatever is inside rattles like broken dishes.

"This is all that's left of Patches!" he says. "I remember Gwennie picking him out at the Canadian Tire, setting him up in the flowerbed. And then you . . . you. . ."

He sits there, flapping his eyebrows, glaring at me, both arms wrapped around his shopping bag.

Patches is a lawn ornament, I figure.

"Please, Mr. Shank," says Darren.

That's the name. I've heard Mom say it.

"Your complaint against Mr. Elegrooter is on record, sir. As you know, Mr. Elegrooter has filed a counter-complaint against you for abusive language."

"Pah!" says Mr. Shank. "He deserved it."

"And damage to the headlight of his rider mower."

"Pah! It was an accident!"

"And attempted assault with a weapon."

"Patches"—I thought he was going to say "Pah" again, but no—"isn't a weapon! He's a garden gnome."

"Apparently," says Darren, "the figure Patches has a pointed hat, which you threatened to, uh, insert in Mr. Elegrooter's—"

"*Ask!*" Mr. Shank points a fat angry finger. "Ask him what he said about Gwennie. Pah! He's a skunk! Pah! A centipede! Pah! A menace!"

With every *pah*, a tiny gob of wetness flies out of his

mouth and lands on the leg of my creased polyester pants. *Who's spitting now?* I'd say, but I'm too relieved. I won't have to spend years behind bars.

It's a busy place, the squad room. The gum-chewing cop at the next desk is on the phone, taking down information about a car. Stolen, I guess. I hear him mention wipers and licence plate, I think. And the colour—red.

I hear Phil's voice from the back of the room. "Did I kill her?" he screams. "Bet I did! Bet I sliced her up. The old bag deserved it!"

"Gentlemen," says Officer Darren, flipping through the pages of the file, "I'll add today's complaints to the file. There's a lot here already."

He runs down a list with his finger, calling out all the things Mr. Shank and I have fought about over the years. Driveway use, visual obstructions, renovations, excavation. I try to imagine two neighbours getting up every morning, wondering how they can make each other's lives wretched.

At the back of the room, in the alcove, Phil's voice rises in a piercing falsetto. He wants everyone to know how bad he is. He's so bad, he doesn't even remember all the bad things he did. Camera? What camera?

I pat my windbreaker pocket. Yup, it's there.

I have some sympathy for Phil—I lived inside his skin, after all—but not much. I already stopped him from stabbing an old woman. That's enough for today.

I have to get out of here. First things first—stand up. This is not as easy as you'd think. Elegrooter uses a walking frame. It's in front of the chair. I bend forward, place my hands on the arms of the frame, and concentrate my strength in my arms. Slowly, swaying, pulling, I lift myself off my seat, leaning forward but keeping a delicate balance. Did I say slowly? It's like building a cathedral. After what seems like a half hour, I achieve my feet, leaning on the walker, panting.

"What's the matter?" Shank asks me. "You running away?"

Running? I can barely walk.

"Maybe," I say.

CHAPTER 24

"Come back!" he shouts.

I keep shuffling.

"Coward!" he shouts.

I keep going.

"Weevil!"

What is it with him and bugs? First he called me a centipede. Now this. I keep walking.

I am not moving fast. I'm not even at the door yet.

"Sorry, Shank," I say over my shoulder. I don't care about winning this argument. I have more important things to think about than his lawn ornament. "Sorry about Patches." What's the wife's name again? "And Gwennie," I say. "Sorry about Gwennie too. She was a fine lady."

My teeth feel funny in my mouth when I smile. I wonder if they're false. I'm at the door.

"I love you, man," I say with a smile.

If Swahili had come out of my mouth, or gold coins, he could not have been more surprised. His eyes are about to roll out of his head. I don't know if I've made him any happier, but sure as salted peanuts I've confused him.

I push the walking frame outside. My aches tumble together like clothes in the dryer. Neck, back, knees, feet, neck again. And there's something wrong with my glasses. When I look down, the world swoops away from me. I almost fall over. When I lift my head, the world comes back.

Yay for wheelchair ramps. Steps would kill me.

There's an overhang in front of the police station. Rain pours off the end of it in a steady stream. I wait for my breathing to slow down. I wonder how Elegrooter got here? They wouldn't let him behind the wheel of a car, would they? He must have taken a cab.

I have to get out of this body. That's the first thing. Maybe I can become somebody cool for a change. Somebody fun. Then I think I'll try and get over to Leon's place. Whether Gord is there or not, Leon will be. And I'd like to see him again.

Wait.

Why do I want to see Leon? Is he gay? Maybe. But what if he isn't? What if I'm not—I mean, what if the me I become next isn't gay?

Though I suspect he will be.

Whatever . . . I'll try to get to 5th Avenue and see what happens.

I fumble the camera out of the windbreaker pocket. I can't read the number. It should be a 7. I hold the camera close and then away, but I can't make it out.

My hands are like claws. I can hardly move them. It is no

fun to be old. I can't find the button on the camera. Is that it? No. Is that? No.

I take deep breaths to calm myself. *Come on, Elegrooter. You can do this, you old coot!* I stand away from the walker so I can use two hands on the camera. Is that the button? I look down, to make sure, and the ground swoops away from me. I put out a hand for balance. And drop the camera.

Damn. It's lying on the sidewalk. I can feel it with my shoe. But I can't bend over and pick it up. I can't even look at it without feeling dizzy. I lean on my walker. I'm so upset I want to scream.

"You okay, mister?"

"Eh?"

I look around for the voice. There, on my left. It's Nikolai. Holy crap, it's Nikolai. I've known him forever.

"You okay?" he says again. "Can I help?"

I feel tears on my cheek. Where did they come from? Frustration? Thanks? I don't know. Nikolai ducks under the overhang to stand beside me. He shakes his lumpy short-cropped head, spraying water droplets.

What a piece of luck.

"Hey, Nikolai!" I say. "I'm glad you're here!"

He lives up the street from me, him and his mom and his brother Ben. We're not friends or anything, because— well, we're not. Nikolai talks slowly and clearly and collects model cars and copies everything the teacher writes on the board. He's that guy. But he's not bad.

"How do you know my name?" he asks me.

"Uhhh. Why, I've known you since you were born, Nikolai."

I'm trying to sound like an old fart. I've heard Nana tell her nurses that.

"Could you get my camera, please?" I ask, pointing downwards, careful not to bend too far over.

"Oh, sure."

He just reaches down and gets it. It takes him a second. Kids don't know how lucky they are. Like elastic bands.

"I want you to take a picture, Nikolai," I say.

"I can try. It might not work. I haven't seen one of these cameras in a long time. I was at a corner store with my aunt Hester three years ago, and I saw one on display. Not this kind, though. It was orange, not green. The corner store was in a strip mall on Westwood Avenue."

See why we're not friends? Nikolai's an okay guy, but he talks like this all the time. Precise, pointed, kind of boring. Funny, because his brother Ben spends his time telling fart jokes and imitating farm animals.

"Here's the button. Do you want me to press it now? I could try to take your picture."

"No, no," I say.

"Or a picture of the street."

"No. It has to be a person. But not me."

Nikolai puts the camera to his eye and swivels his head around. This wet block of King Street is empty. The lights in front of the town hall turn yellow and then red for nobody. Across the street are shops offering shoes and antiques and haircuts. No one is buying.

"I don't see anybody to take a picture of," says Nikolai.

"How about a picture of yourself, then?" I say. "You're a

cool guy." Of course, Nikolai is not cool. But he's not old and decrepit. He can walk. He can run. "Sure." I nod. "Why not take a picture of yourself?"

"I'm not that cool," he says. "I mean, I'm not Ryan Brady."

"Who? Oh, him."

He's a guy from our town who made it to the NHL—Vancouver, I think. But he played for the Buzzards just a couple of years ago. The local paper has a headline every time he scores a goal. *Dresden Native Ryan Brady* is the way they refer to him.

"He's really cool," says Nikolai.

"Take a picture of yourself," I say. "Please do it. Do it now. Do it for me."

And now I sound like a creepy old man. Ew. But before Nikolai realizes this, he gets distracted. There's a car at the intersection of King and George, a block away. The engine revs really loud.

Nikolai still has the camera up. He turns towards the car. And what a car! It's red and low-slung, knife-edged and glistening in the rain, with a grille like the mouth of a shark.

"Now *that's* cool," Nikolai whispers.

He's right.

The light changes. With a mighty *blat* from oversized exhaust pipes, the shark-mouthed machine races towards us. Nikolai tracks it with the camera.

And sends me to paradise.

DAN'L

CHAPTER 25

The feeling doesn't last long, but I plan to remember it to my dying day. For the first time in my life, I am behind the wheel of a car. No, not a car. A dream.

Technically, it's a Dodge Viper—bright red paint, black leather upholstery, and a speedometer that goes up to 330 kilometers an hour. Yes, 330. I know. Even the wiper blades move fast. The rain has no chance. The automatic shifter on the floor oozes with power. The dashboard gleams and flashes. The sound system pumps out block-rocking beats.

And me? I'm wearing driving gloves that are as soft and supple as a second skin, and a black leather vest with fringes. The mirror shows me in a cowboy hat with a long brim and a low crown. My chin is long and firm. My eyes are covered, despite the grey day, by the coolest sunglasses in history. Oh, and I have a cell phone looped around my ear. I look about eighteen. Either I have a heckuva summer job, or I'm rich. I am, for all intents and purposes, a Master of the Universe.

I can move all my muscles with ease. Whew! Do all old people feel as bad as Elegrooter? I hope not. Nana sounds chirpy when Mom and I visit the Golden Years Villa, even if she doesn't know our names.

So I'm driving the world's fastest car, wearing incredible clothes, and *not* hurting. To think I would have settled for being Nikolai. This me is way cooler.

There is a minor hiccup when I try to stop for the red light at Hibernia Street. I hit the brake hard, and the car skids. I had Magnus's reflexes, and Elegrooter's, and now I have this guy's. Master of the Universe but a lousy driver. The car keeps skidding. Oh-oh.

Time slows down, and I see the future spooling away like a dropped roll of toilet paper. I'll skid into the intersection and get T-boned by a teenager taking the family dog to the vet. Trapped, I'll need the Jaws of Life to get out, and then the dog will bite me—and turn out to have rabies . . .

The intersection is empty. I end up with the Viper's nose pointing up Hibernia Street. I give the accelerator a touch with my foot, just enough to take me to the next intersection. The light's red, and I stop easily. When the light changes, I turn right again. Legally this time.

Oh, *yeah.*

The rain is letting up. I shut off the windshield wipers first try.

"Hey!" I say aloud. Getting a bit of confidence back. "Hey, I can do this." I have a husky voice, I find. And a bit of an accent, like I'm from the South. (*Ah kin do this.*)

Man, I am the bomb.

I want this life. My new one. My *real* one.

"Kinda cool." I say it out loud and smile into the mirror. Whoever I am, thank you.

Could I stay in this life forever? Is that what Gord meant when he said the camera was for me—that I was to find who I wanted to be? Because I feel really good right now. But I can't help wondering about my body—I mean, my old one. What's going on with it? Does Gord know? I hope so. Maybe I should get over to 5th Avenue.

Sure. That's what I'll do. I'll find Gord, tell him I want *this* life.

I'm getting the hang of my new reflexes. The car is under control, heading up William. The rain has stopped. I'll go to Elgin and then over to 5th. Busy music now, repetitive, hypnotic. Listening to it feels like driving in a dark tunnel, lights flashing by. Robin Rich is playing hopscotch on the sidewalk outside her dad's car dealership. She's in my class at school. An athletic girl, a loner. Short hair, braces, socks, and shorts. She squints at my car. Who is he? she wonders.

Who am I? I'm someone who can honk at a hopscotching girl.

You never can tell, can you? When I think how much my outlook on life has improved in, like, a half hour, I am amazed. Nobody knows the future, but right now things are good.

Tim Hortons and McDonald's on my left, parkland on my right. The sun is shining from behind a thin layer of cloud so that everything looks bright but hazy. I steer easily through the light traffic.

There's a click in my ear and a woman's voice.

"Dan'l?" she says. "Dan'l, are you there? It's me, Jan."

Good to know my name.

"Uh, hi there," I say. (It comes out *Hah theah*. I bite my tongue not to giggle.) "How are things with you, Jan?"

"Did you get the car?"

She has a smooth voice, Jan does. Like olive oil, pouring golden into the pan. Sounds like she and Dan'l are good friends. Maybe more than friends. Like, maybe Dan's not gay. And if he's not gay, maybe I'm not either.

What about that? How much am I Dan, and how much am I me?

"I'm driving right now."

First time in my life I've said that. I thought I'd have to wait another three years. This is a proud moment.

"A Viper, like you promised? Dan'l, you're amazing!"

I'm coming up to the five-way traffic lights at Elgin Avenue. Green turns to yellow. I slow to a smooth halt. I'm behind a Volkswagen. On my left is the park where Magnus played basketball, and so did I, as Magnus.

And then my life changes. Again. It only takes a word.

"Where'd you steal it from?" Jan asks.

"Steal?"

That's the word.

"I'll phone Hope Springs now. You get there as soon as you can. Pull in the back of the garage, like usual." She hangs up.

A chorus line of centipedes rehearses on my backbone.

CHAPTER 26

take a quick look down. The Viper comes with a push-button ignition. No key. A piece of the dash has been ripped off underneath, and there's wires hanging out, thin filaments of yellow and red and brown. The car has been hot-wired.

So I am not a Master of the Universe. I'm a crook. And I'm driving a car as conspicuous as a parade float. How thin is the line between fantasy and mess, cool and lame, fun and yuck.

And it takes only seconds for the yuck to get yuckier. The light is still red. Two cars pull up and stop in the lane next to mine. One is a grey minivan. The other is a black sedan with the word *Police* in gold lettering on the side.

Oh, snap.

I have a vivid memory of the officer on the phone back at the police station. He wasn't talking about *wipers,* I realize. It was *Viper*—a stolen car description. *Uh-huh, radiant red,* he said.

I hold my hand up to my head, keeping an eye on the cop through my fingers. Her mouth is moving. Is she talking to the dispatcher? Is she calling in the licence plate? I moan in time with the pulses of the music. "Oh, no. Oh oh, no. Oh oh oh, no."

The minivan driver smiles widely and gives me a thumbs-up. He likes the car.

At last the light changes. The Volkswagen in front of me pulls ahead sedately. I put on my right turn signal and pull forward. Will I get away?

Nope.

I'm halfway through the turn onto Elgin Street when I hear a *bleep* from beside me. The cop turns from the wrong lane, staying with me. Her lights are flashing. She motions me to the side of the road.

The camera sticks out of the top pocket of my leather vest. It calms me. The idea comes smoothly, naturally, like swallowing a gulp of water. I'll wait for the cop to come to my window and take her picture. Then, as the cop, I'll let Dan'l off with a warning. He'll drive away, and I can head to 5th Avenue in the cop car. I've got plenty of pictures left—five, I think. If nothing goes wrong.

I steer to the side of the road. I have time to notice that the Best Western Hotel down the street is welcoming minor atom hockey players, that the girl walking her dog on the other side of Elgin Street has a giant pimple on her cheek like mine this morning. The cop *bleeps* her siren again. She's in my lane now. Her flashing lights are in my rear-view mirror. I stomp on the brake. Only it's not the brake pedal I hit. It's the accelerator. The car takes off. Oops.

Wow, is my car fast! I cover the whole block in about a

second, and then I'm at the next intersection. I'm horrified, of course. I'm in way more trouble with the cops now. But I'm also gleeful. I'm flying down Elgin Street.

The light at 1st Avenue is red—but so what? No one's around. I don't lift my foot. Feels like I'm being sucked ahead by a giant tractor beam.

If I stop now and give myself up, I'm afraid the cop will grab me before I can take her picture. So I don't stop. Another intersection: 2nd Avenue. I pull around an SUV as though it's standing still. The cop car is way behind me, siren blaring, lights flashing in my rear-view.

A ray of sunshine angles through the cloudbank on my left like a searchlight. Time pole-vaults over space, and 3rd Avenue is behind me before I know it. The houses are smaller now, closer together. Cars with For Sale signs on them sit on lawns with For Sale signs on *them*.

The streets are named 1st, 2nd, 3rd, but the next is written out—Forth. Forth Avenue. I don't know if that's a joke or if the Dresden town fathers couldn't spell. The light at Forth is red, and there are cars on both sides, waiting. I pull into the oncoming lane and make an illegal left turn. There's a noise like girls screaming at a birthday party. My tires.

The neighbourhood off Forth Avenue above Elgin is known as The Junction. If there's a bar fight in Dresden or Hope Springs, odds are that one or both of the fighters will be from The Junction. The street heads uphill steeply. My car doesn't care. Ravine on my right, houses on my left. I take the left turn at the top of the hill, then a quick right, then another right.

Houses on this street are rickety. Broken steps, boarded windows, missing shingles. Dalton lives around here. He's in my class at school. A tough guy. Dirty fingernails, heavy boots, stories of rats and guns. Of course, he also claims to party with Drake and Jennifer Lawrence and what's-her-name from *Family Guy*. You can't believe Dalton.

I swoop around an S bend and almost run over a couple walking along the drainage ditch. Do I know the girl? I stare a second too long and lose control of the car. I brake, skid, spin one and a half times, and head towards the ditch. Down goes my hood. Up goes the back end. The car tips and slides until the front grille rests on the squishy wet bottom of the ditch. I put the car in reverse and try to back up and out. Nothing happens.

CHAPTER 27

slide out. The car is angled like a thrown javelin, hood and front wheels in the ditch, back in the air. No damage, but it's not going anywhere.

Doreen comes over. She's who I was staring at, why I lost control of the car. Doreen from the cinnamon place at the mall. I guess she lives up here. It's a long-ish walk for her.

"Hi, Doreen," I say. *Do-rayne* is how it comes out.

Except that, up close and with the hoodie down, this isn't her. It's not a girl at all.

"You know my sister?" he asks me.

I nod. I remember her talking about her brother. "You're Eli, right?"

He looks like Doreen, if she were a guy. Seriously cute. Jutting chin, bony shoulders.

The guy who was walking with Eli comes over now. He was checking out the underside of my car. No way you'd think this guy was a girl—he's big and bulgy.

"How do you know Doreen?" he says intensely. "She's my business." Then he blinks.

"Oh, hi, Dan'l," he says. "I didn't recognize you right away."

I nod.

"So that Viper in the ditch is the one Jan phoned about," he says. "Lucky you didn't wreck it. I'll call for a tow now."

He's about Dan'l's age, or Phil's—late teens. His neck tattoo might look cool on some guys but not him. It says *HOT STUFF*. He's got jowls, so the letters droop and it's hard to read.

Seriously. *HOT STUFF*?

Could he be Doreen's ex-boyfriend? She called him a ---- jerk. And this guy seems like one.

"So you know Dave," Eli says to me.

Dave. That was the name. I nod.

Dave's got his cell phone to his ear, calling his dad for a tow.

"You steal cars for him, eh?" says Eli with a grin. "Dave's my best friend. So if you work for him, you and me are cool too. I can boost old cars now, and I'm learning how to do the new ones. How hard was it to get that Viper started?"

I take off my sunglasses. He's eager, like a kid. A mean kid.

"You're not like your sister, are you?" I say. "You look like her, but—"

"Oh, Doreen is so boring. She works at the mall making cinnamon buns. She's not cool."

We're not alone, Eli and Dave and I. A flipped sports car is news in this neighbourhood. Lawns and porches are filling. Bikes stop. Fingers point. Tongues flap. Camera phones flash.

A girl pushing a stroller with a wriggly baby in it slows

down to take in the sight. The baby tries to climb out. The girl grabs the baby just in time. I recognize the girl. So does Dave. He puts away his phone and shouts at her.

"Hey, Doreen!"

She's wearing a cap with a brim, like a sea captain or an old hippie. Her hair is mostly tucked underneath.

"C'mere, Doreen!" Dave shouts again. "Come and say hi."

She looks up with a frown.

"I'm busy, Dave. Babysitting."

"I said, c'mere!"

"And I said, I'm busy!"

Dave turns to me. "How do you like that girl? She's feisty, isn't she? Wonder how she'd like to—?" He breaks off.

"Oh-oh," he says.

Three cop cars skid around the corner and stop near the upended Viper. Officers pile out. I wonder how they got here so quick. Someone must have sent a picture.

Dave's eyebrows make a thick V in the middle of his forehead. "You're in it now," he says to me. "The cops want that car. If they get you, don't say nothing."

"You mean, don't talk about you?"

"Shut up."

"And car stealing?"

"*Shut up.*"

There's so much, what, yuckiness in the words, so much venom, that he sounds like my brother Ray. I shudder. I really do.

I do not want handcuffs on me before I can snap a picture. I barely got out of jail last time, and I'm not going back.

In the top pocket of my leather vest is the camera. I take it out and hold it loose in my hand. It's my way out of here. It calms me. And with the calm comes an idea. I like Doreen and I don't like Dave. Doreen doesn't like Dave either. My idea will help her get away from him.

"Hey, officers," I call out. "That's my car in the ditch there."

The rain has stopped but there are still a few clouds up there. They look like pads of steel wool—fuzzy, rounded, gray, tough. Scouring clouds.

A cop steps towards me. It's the one who pulled me over. The uniform suits her, belt and boots. And gun. She pulls it fast. The gun, I mean.

"You!" she shouts.

My hands are on my head. "I want to make a statement," I say loudly. "My name is Dan'l and I stole that Dodge Viper. I work with a garage in Hope Springs. The garage is owned by Dave's dad. That's Dave over there, with the HOT STUFF tattoo." I keep one hand on my head, point with the other. "I can name names," I say. "Dave can too. You should take him in."

The hand I use to point at Dave is the one with the camera in it.

Lots of things happen.

Doreen is nodding as I talk, as if she suspected something about Dave all along. When she sees the camera in my hand her jaw drops.

Meanwhile, the tough policewoman tells Dave to stand still.

He's sliding backwards. "I'll get you, Dan'l," he says.

Meanwhile, two more cops run over.

Under all this movement, the crowd on the street and lawns is going *Oooh* and *Ahhh* and *Did you hear?* as a sort of background music. An older guy, scrawny, in an undershirt and shorts, with frizzed hair, walks to the edge of the front porch of the house nearest to the upended car and leans forward with his hands on the railing.

"Hey-oh, daughter!" he shouts to Doreen. "What the ---- is going on?"

He has a voice like a cracked church bell. Huge, magnificent, spit-flawed.

"What does it ---- look like?" she shouts back. "Stolen cars, what else?"

I can't see any resemblance between Doreen and her dad. But I can hear it.

"Is that ---- boyfriend of yours part of this?" he shouts.

"He's not my ---- boyfriend!" she shouts back, her mouth wide enough for me to see her chewing gum.

"What about your brother? He involved?"

"What about me, old man?" shouts Eli.

"You stealing cars, boy?"

"---- no!" shouts Eli.

The Mormons should get in on this, I think. *The family that swears together, cares together,* or something. Dave is out of sight now, back in the crowd. Two cops are running after him. I hope they catch him and put him away.

"Bye," I say to Doreen.

I've got to work fast before the police take me away. I bring the camera up to my face. There's a kid with a bike standing next to Doreen. I'll take his picture, then ride down to Leon's place. That's a warm thought.

Doreen swears. The bike kid in my viewfinder moves suddenly, diving to the pavement with his arms out, like a wide receiver. I swing the camera after him and click the shutter. Doreen swears again. I'm gone.

KAREN

CHAPTER 28

Can you guess? The kid dropped his bike and dove to save the baby who was trying to climb out of the stroller again. In the same second, Doreen reached down to help and my shutter clicked.

I am not the bike kid. Too bad, because he's clearly a good guy.

I'm not Doreen either.

Yeah, that's right. I'm the baby. Not an infant, more like a toddler. Two years old, maybe. I bet I can walk okay, which is why I keep trying to climb out of the stroller. I want to show everyone what I can do.

Damn!

Right now I'm being held at arms' length by the wide receiver kid, who is lying on the ground on his back. I'm directly over his face, which, by the way, is pretty clean. I see soap film at his hairline. He must have just washed.

"Karen!" yells Doreen, grabbing me from above and behind and hoiking me into the air. "What are you doing?

You are one ---- crazy baby, you know that?" She holds me facing away from her.

"Say thank you to Max!" she tells me. Then, "Thanks, Max, those are some ---- fast reflexes. You saved Karen here a bump on the head!"

Max scrambles away, wiping his face with his sleeve. I may have drooled on him.

Karen? So I'm a girl again. Doesn't matter that much. I'm in a diaper, and a diaper is a unisex bathroom.

Across the road, a handsome guy is moaning. "Oh, my! Oh, lordy, no! Oh, my my my!" *Oh, ma.*

That's Dan'l, who has seen the Viper in the ditch. His face crumples like paper. He squeezes his cowboy hat.

"That beautiful car! I must have blacked out. Did I crash?" *Did ah cray-ash?*

I may never sound that hilarious again. The policewoman leads him away. Poor guy, he doesn't know what he's admitted, how much trouble he's in. He pats the rear bumper of the Viper on his way past. It's like he's saying he's sorry to the car.

Poor guy? Maybe not. He is a thief, after all, which is not that cool. I put him out of my mind and concentrate on me. I'm in trouble too.

Doreen holds me tight. She's enormous, by the way. Her ear is bigger than my whole hand.

There's something sticking into my side, but I can't get at it. Remember how I had Magnus's reflexes and then Dan'l's? Well, now I am in this baby's body, and there's lots of stuff I can't do. Babies are pretty incompetent.

"Put me down!" I say.

Of course, it doesn't come out like that, because I am a baby. But I do manage a couple of words—sounds like, *Put down.*

Doreen brings me around to her front, holds me so I face her. "Karen!" she says. "Listen to you! Who's a smart girl? Okay, I'll put you in the stroller, but you have to stay there!"

So she does. I am facing forward now.

"Thank you," I say. And something very like those words comes out.

"Wow! What good manners! Wait till I tell Daddy. What a ---- polite girl you are!"

"You betcha." That doesn't come out right at all.

We stroller away down towards Forth Avenue. A cruiser passes us. Dan'l is in the back seat.

I wriggle around, trying to get at whatever is digging into my side. I can guess what it is, but I can't reach it. Come on, arm! Stretch yourself. Stretch! Being a baby is going to delay me getting to 5th Avenue.

Finally! I get a hand into my sweat pants and feel cardboard. As I thought, it's the camera. Now, pull!

Nothing.

Pull again!

My fingers slip.

Grip harder and pull!

Nothing. Nothing.

The camera is stuck in my waistband. Damn damn damn.

This is serious. How am I going to get down to 5th Avenue? How am I going to get anywhere? Babies are good at getting attention, but they don't know what to do with it. At least Elegrooter could talk.

I pull at the camera again.

There's no sidewalk on the other side of the street. The trees come right to the pavement. Maple trees, mostly, with some evergreens and a few silver birch gleaming like a promise between the darker trunks. The leaves are starting to turn.

I pull and pull. Nothing.

Stupid camera. Stupid baby hands. I'm mad enough to scream. So I do.

But underneath the anger, I'm scared. What if I can't get the camera out, don't take another picture? What if . . . I'm Karen forever? I tell myself I will not waste any more time. If I get out of this mess, I will run to 5th Avenue.

I wonder if that's always true, about anger? Underneath, is everybody scared? I twist like a pretzel and wave my hands and scream like a banshee.

We stop. Doreen comes round and squats, her head at my level.

"Karen! Karen! What the ---- is going on with you?"

When she sees what I'm grabbing at, her laughter stops like it has run into a wall.

CHAPTER 29

Doreen holds the disposable camera away from me. Armies of confusion march and countermarch across her face. But that camera isn't hers. It's—

"Mine!" The word rolls off my tongue. It must be one of those words that all little kids know how to say, like *no* and *mama*.

"I saw one of these camera a couple of minutes ago," Doreen says. "That friend of Dave's had it. Looked just like this. There was one in the mall, too. A lot of these ---- cameras around today."

"Mine."

Doreen knows something weird is going on and that this camera is part of it. I want to tell her how she can help me. *Take a picture of someone, so I can get out of Karen's body.* But Karen's working vocabulary is really small. I have to simplify. This reminds me of French class. The hero of our storybook, Armand, seems to be about eighteen years old, but he speaks like he's in Grade 3. *Good afternoon,* he says. *It is windy. My dog is very large. My car has a pain in the tire.*

I have to think like Armand here. Keep it simple.

"Take a picture," I say.

Picture comes out *bibber*. Damn. Doreen frowns, and I try again.

"Click!" I say, practically strangling myself. "No—snap!" Only it comes out *nap*.

"Do you want a nap?" she says. "Is it nap time?"

"No no no!" I say. "No nap. No no."

And now I sound like every other kid in the world.

"---- !" I say. The word comes out pretty good, which makes sense if Karen's been listening to Doreen.

"You don't sound like yourself, honey," she says.

I nod vigorously. I'll bet I know how to say my own name. I take a deep breath.

"Not Karen," I say. "Me not Karen!"

Whew!

Doreen gasps.

I point at the camera. "Bibber!" No, no. I try again. "Fodo!" Not bad. Karen can certainly make an *f* sound. "Take fodo! Take fodo. Please!" I say.

"Photo?" says Doreen. "Did you say *photo*?"

I nod vigorously. "Fodo! Fodo!"

Doreen looks scared. "You and the ---- camera. What's going on?"

She moves away from me as if I'm possessed or something. Which, you know, is not far off the truth. *Me not Karen.* It is kind of freaky, isn't it?

"Do you want a picture of yourself?"

She moves back and puts the camera to her eye.

"No!" I yell. Why would I want a picture of Karen? I don't want to be Karen.

Mind you, if I was a girl, I'd have an easier time with boys. Because I like boys.

There seems to be no getting away from myself. That program's been running in the background all the time. No matter who I am, I like boys. I'm scared of that but relieved too. Relieved to know the truth, to know who I am. A few minutes ago, I was noticing Eli. He's a cute guy. Yeah, he's a loser, hanging out with Dave—but he's a cute loser.

"No," I say again, waving my hands in front of my face. "No me fodo. No please no." I don't want to be Karen. And I don't want any more wasted shots.

Now I notice a guy running past. His arms move like clockwork. His feet skim the pavement. He's dressed in shorts and a tight-fitting shirt, with a headband to keep the sweat out of his eyes. He checks his wrist, then peers back over his shoulder at something behind us.

Doreen is still holding the camera. If she won't take a picture, I'll try. I wonder if Karen can say *Gimme*.

"Gimme!"

Yup.

"Gimme! Gimme! Gimme!"

I clamber to my feet, using my hands to get myself up. The stroller seat is flat and firm. I lunge forward, grabbing the camera in my little hands, but one foot gets caught in the soft webbing of the seat, and I fall sideways out of the stroller.

Time slows down, and I picture my head hitting the pavement, blotting out memory and some brain function. I'll end up spending the rest of my life as Karen, with thick glasses and dirty fingernails, not knowing anything about a magic camera. My boyfriend will be a creep named Marvin, who tortures animals and has a knife collection. Sheesh!

Here I am in the horrible future shop again. Why do I keep coming here? Is there a sale?

Fortunately, before any of this can happen, Doreen catches me around the waist and swings me up. I'm facing away from her, holding the camera tight. Now is my moment! I push the shutter. Nothing happens. I can't do it. My fingers aren't strong enough. I try again. Fail again.

My scream is an explosion born of frustration. Babies must often feel like this—their ambition is so much greater than their ability. A typical baby wants to destroy the world a few times a day. I open my entire face and produce one of those epic soul-emptying, stomach-shrivelling shrieks.

Doreen's not impressed. She's heard it before. She holds me firmly on her hip with one hand and reaches for the camera. Her hand beside mine is rougher, darker, and enormous. The camera points away from us. We push together on the shutter.

JULIUS

CHAPTER 30

'm hovering! How is this possible? I'm positively floating along, just off the ground, propelled forward on a cushion of air. No, wait. I'm doing it myself. I'm running. One at a time, my feet touch the pavement and take off again, left, right, left, landing on the heel and rolling forward to spring off the toe. Each step is light—a breath, no more. I am the wind. I am motion.

And speaking of breath, I had no idea that lungs could work like this. In through the nose *two three four five six*, and out through the mouth *two three four* . . . No labour, no stress, no puffing or panting. The distance simply vanishes. I move like fire along a fuse, eating up the block. Who could imagine that running would be so easy, so effortless, so much fun?

What a relief to not be a toddler anymore!

Behind me, Doreen is trying to put Karen in the stroller, and Karen is having none of it. She clings like a barnacle. Poor little kid, confused and scared and I don't know what. Doreen ends up carrying her in one arm, pushing the stroller with her free hand. I think about going after her and explaining—but how to do that without sounding crazy?

And I must get to 5th Avenue. The more I think about that, the more it makes sense. I'll grab Gord and make him tell me what he knows. And I'll get a chance to talk to Leon while I'm there. Talk to him without bars between us. That'd be amazing.

He's the only one who knows *what* I am—and he doesn't know *who* I am.

All this time I've been running. I'm at the top of the hill looking down to Elgin Street. Ravine on my left, Junction on my right. Without pausing, I drink from the water bottle in my mesh belt. The wind is blowing the grey away bit by bit, and the sun bleeds through. Beyond Elgin I see a couple of church spires and the flat, infinite horizon of the great lake in the distance. I've known it forever.

In *two three four five six*, out *two three* . . . I don't count on purpose—I just find myself doing it. Whoever I am is in astoundingly good shape, and you don't get that way unless you think about it all the time.

The camera is in one of the pouches in the utility belt. Three pictures left. Three chances to get—well, wherever I'm supposed to get. Is that scary? Kind of.

And speaking of scary, I see another runner on Elgin Street, coming towards Forth. I freeze. He turns onto Forth and waves up at me. What should I do? I can't think. I can't think at all.

Like me, this guy is young, fit, wearing running gear. I take a breath. I must have stopped breathing the moment I saw who it was.

He runs up with a smile on his face. "Julius!" he says. "You got here first this time. You must have started ahead of me. No way you could have beat me. We both know that, right?"

My throat's dry. I take another swig of water and greet my brother.

Yes, it's Ray. I've seen those blue shorts folded on top of the laundry pile regularly for months. The smile is new, though. He doesn't smile at me this way. I remember Julius now. He's a running friend of Ray's, usually dressed in tight clothes and a wide kerchief-style headband. Which I am wearing now. Julius has been by the house a few times but has never come in.

I'm angry and scared, but numb too. Numb is like ice on top of the river of feelings.

"I'll go first," says Ray. "When you go first, I have to slow up, and I hate to do that."

He's teasing Julius—light teasing, but it's still hard to take. He cuts into the woods, shouts over his shoulder at me to follow. Which I do because—because—because of a few things.

First, because he's my big brother, and I'm used to doing what he says. I hate him—yeah, I do—but I seem to lose power when I'm around him.

One time—this is a strong memory—I broke a piece from his castle set. A catapult or something. I knocked it off the table and it broke. Ray got so mad his face went bunchy and lumpy. He told me he *hated* me and that I was a loser.

"And you'll *always* be a loser," he said.

I was devastated by the hate and the *always*. I told him he could break my favourite toy to make up for me wrecking his catapult. He thought that was a good idea. So we went down to the basement together, and he took a hammer to my helicopter with the rotating blade. I can see him holding the heavy tool with both hands, bringing it up over his head and down onto the red plastic, again and again. He'd be, what, eight? Nine, maybe. It was cool in the basement, light filtering through the small dirty windows set high on the wall.

"Now am I a loser?" I asked. I stared at the pieces on the cement floor and tried not to cry.

"Yes," he said.

What I meant was, are we even? And it seemed that we weren't.

"What if you smash another toy?" I asked. "Will I still be a loser?"

"I don't know," he said.

I went up to my room and picked a Mega Man action figure from my toy chest. Funny the things you remember. I brought Mega Man down to the basement, and Ray smashed him too.

"Loser?" I said.

"Yes."

The two of us carried my toy chest down to the basement, and Ray smashed his way through it, toy by toy. He couldn't smash the stuffed animals, but he pulled them apart. The only thing he couldn't ruin was a model of a blue whale from the museum gift shop. Man, that thing was tough. Ray twisted it, pulled it, hit it a bunch of times, but it wouldn't come apart.

When the chest was empty, he swept the bits of plastic and metal and wood and stuffing into a bag and told me to carry it out to the garage. And I did, because he said so.

Pathetic? Yes. But that's one reason why I follow him now. Habit.

Second, and more important, Ray is part of today. If there's a plan for me, as Gord says there is, then there's a *reason* why things are happening this way. When I was Lisa, I found out about me and about Magnus. When I was Phil, I met Leon and found out where he and Gord live. Now I'm Julius, and I'm going to find out about Ray—or—wait a minute.

Wait just a minute.

I have an idea. And w*hat* an idea. It's wonderful and awful and fully formed even now at its birth. I hug it to me, my idea.

I follow him along the path and down the hill. The woods are bright with colour, a few leaves beginning to turn but most of them still fresh and green. He picks his way neatly. He's good at small finicky things. He always knifes up the right amount of butter to put on his bread, and measures out exact amounts of paper and ribbon for his Christmas presents.

I hear water noise below us, getting louder as we descend. Usually the Dresden River is as calm as pudding and knee-shallow, but it races along today, full of mud and junk.

Ray sets off upstream. This must be a regular route for him and Julius. No one's around. The muddy path beside the river is just wide enough for the two of us.

We round a clump of bushes and come to a straight stretch. Ray picks up the pace. I do too. I pass him. He passes me. I pass him back. And soon we are racing hard.

Up ahead of us, a big old tree has fallen across the river, making a bridge. That's our finish line—I know it.

I'd never be able to beat Ray as myself, but Julius is a way better runner. *In two* out *two* in *two* out *two*. Ray falls behind. For once in our lives, I'm going faster than he is. I have Julius's talent and my own desire. I focus on the tree. I can beat Ray to it. I can. In *two* out *two*. I can fly. I can—

Ray trips me. He throws out his front foot to catch my trailing one, and when he kicks up, I fall head-first. One minute I'm flying along, the next I'm on the ground with a muddy front. He keeps going to the tree trunk, slaps it with the flat of his hand, and turns to smile at me.

"Good race," he says in a low voice. "Too bad you fell."

"You tripped me! You were losing, and you tripped me. Cheater."

"*Cheater,*" he mimics. "*Cheater cheater cheater!* You sound like my brother, Jonah, complaining to Mom."

I'm angry but I don't say anything. Not yet. I hug my idea. Watch out, Ray.

The tree trunk bridge is about as wide as a ladder but not stable. It creaks as I get on. I reposition my feet, gripping hard on the rounded sides. Bare branches trail in the rushing water. Roots stick up like broken fingers reaching through prison bars. The river rushes under me, carrying all sorts of stuff—small branches, garbage, pieces of clothing, who knows what.

Ray's halfway across, moving easily, arms spread wide.

It's time. I take out the camera and call his name. He looks back with that mocking smile I know as well as my own hand.

"Ray, Ray, you are in such trouble," I say.

"What?"

"Bad things are going to happen to you, Ray. In a few seconds, you'll black out, and when you wake up, you'll be in a giant mess."

This is my idea. This is why I'm here. I'm going to become Ray and then—carefully and completely—wreck his life. He'll wonder why all these horrors (I haven't decided which ones) have happened to him—why he's naked in front of the town hall, say. Or why his room is covered in garbage. Or how the fire started. I picture him shivering, infected, confused, and crying. I picture him sick and scared and totally alone.

Wow, am I ever mad at him. My idea offers a chance to get back at him for the helicopter and Mega Man and—and—everything. Today has been leading up to this moment. *For you*, said Gord. This moment is for me.

My brother turns carefully to face me, hands on his hips, head cocked to one side.

"What are you *talking* about, Julius?"

"You don't know, do you, Ray? You don't know *anything*. You don't even know who I am."

The river hurtles by, a confusion of grey foam, green water, debris, danger. My mind is in a similar state. I lift the camera. My brother's face fills the viewfinder, staring out at me. My finger hovers over the button. I think about what my plan means. Not what I'll *do* when I'm Ray, but the second of

149

actually *becoming* him, sliding my soul into his body, breathing his breath, sweating his sweat, seeing the world out his eye-holes.

And.

And.

And I can't do it. Just flat-out can't.

After the toy box thing I kind of gave up on Ray. I stopped following him around, didn't want anything more to do with him. Didn't care about him. And I still don't.

Maybe I should have tried to like him. Or at least to understand. I mean, maybe he's really unhappy. Maybe he's scared of something. Maybe life is hard for him in some way I don't get.

But it's hard to sympathize with the bully's sore toe when he's kicking you with it.

I don't want to become Ray, not even to wreck his life. It'd be like climbing into filthy underwear.

I pause. And in that pause, Ray turns un-carefully back around, loses his footing on the log, and falls into the river. The rushing torrent of green closes over him, and he's gone.

CHAPTER 31

Here's another memory—a quick one. The first time I went on the Zipper I wasn't tall enough, according to the sign, and Mom would have said no, but I was with Nana, who said we'd ask. And the ride operator—he had a snake tattoo stretching up one arm and around his neck—shrugged and said, *Sure, kid.* This was the July 1st long weekend, and the Dresden pier had been turned into a mini amusement park. Rides and fast food, ring toss and shooting games, and the throb and stink of portable generators. It was sunny, that day. In my memory, carnival weekend is always sunny.

Do you know the Zipper? You're locked in a small cage that spins and somersaults along an elliptical track, like an orbit. The effect is cosmic. After thirty seconds, you have no idea of up or down, true or false, past or future. And everything has fallen out of your pockets.

When I staggered out of my Zipper cage my first time, I was pleased and satisfied. And then I smelled the diesel and frying onions, and nausea hit me like a swinging door.

That's almost exactly what happens now. There's a gut-deep satisfaction in Ray going into the river. *Oh, yeah!* And then he doesn't surface, and doesn't surface, and doesn't surface, and I stare downstream and feel sick to my stomach.

How can this be? Just a few seconds ago, I was mad enough at my brother to want to ruin his entire future. And suddenly as a coin flip, a different feeling overwhelms me. I'm worried about him. The river is full and fast, and if he gets caught or knocks his head against something, he might, well, drown.

What happened? Why should I care about him? He's the same bully, and I'm the same victim.

Or am I? I don't know. There's lots I don't know. But this I'm sure of. In the same way I couldn't *become* Ray, I can't watch him drown and do nothing. I just can't.

I dive in after him.

The water is too murky to see through. I feel around ahead of me, and after a few anxious seconds I get hold of his arm. I pull him to the surface and find that I can stand up. The water is up to my chest. I hang onto Ray's arm to hold him up. The current tugs at us. He flails around with his free hand, clawing at himself. There's an animal—a hairy creepy stretchy thing—attached to his far shoulder.

"Get it off me!" he shouts.

I try to help, but the thing is strong and sticky. It hangs on.

Ray screams at me to *please please get it off.*

I wonder if it's one of those huge spiders. I've seen pictures of them, big as a dinner plate. Is it a rat? A cat? A skunk? Is it—?

There's a firm flat rock under my feet. I step up onto it, and the river level drops to my waist. Now I can see better. I shake my head, blink the water out of my eyes, and start to laugh. I pluck the hairy thing off Ray and hold it so he can see it too.

The water rushes past us. Ray closes his eyes for a second. His whole face turns poppy red.

"Oh," he says.

It's a scarf.

That's right, a length of knitted love, floating downstream on the flood. It looks like some kind of slime, and probably felt like a creepy animal when it was around Ray's neck. But it's *a scarf.*

"You okay now?" I ask him.

"I lost my balance. I was choking."

"And that was a *nasty* piece of wool, eh? Scary!"

"Shut up, Julius!"

"Good thing Nana didn't make you one for Christmas—you'd scream, and she'd feel bad."

"Shut up!" he says. "Don't you dare tell anybody."

We make our way back to the tree trunk bridge and hoist ourselves out of the water. I can't help it—it's been a long day, and I'm tired. I laugh and laugh. I can't stand, I'm laughing so hard. And Ray has to take it. He shakes his head and says we've got to be going.

"Let's finish our run," he says. "We'll go together. If I go first, you'll never catch up, you slowpoke."

He's trying to tease like usual, to show me who's boss. I picture him with the wet scarf, throw back my head, and laugh some more.

Why, oh *why*, haven't I been able to laugh at Ray before? I guess it's tough to laugh at a bully. And he doesn't make a lot of mistakes. Neat, tidy, fast, busy. It's hard to laugh at that. And he's older. And I wanted him to like me. And I was an easy victim.

Yeah, it was my fault too.

I get to my feet.

"How did you know about Nana?" he asks. "That's what we call her, and she likes to knit. How did you know that, Julius?"

I think about him finding out that his little brother likes guys. Will he tease me? Will he laugh? Sure. But I'll picture him in the river, fighting off the fearful scarf, and I'll laugh right back. Maybe I will.

What can he do about it? And how much will I care?

I don't know.

"Your nana's been good to me," I tell him.

She saw me staggering away from the Zipper that time. She hurried over and put her arm around me. I desperately didn't want to vomit all over the crowd, but I couldn't keep it in. My jaw locked, the way it does just before everything comes up. Nana saw all this. Without hesitating, she opened her big cloth handbag and let me throw up in it. No muss, no fuss, no bother. When I was done, she tossed her bag into a garbage bin and walked to the park. I felt way better and told her how sorry I was. She told me not to worry and ruffled my hair, plastic bracelets clacking.

"What about your bag?" I asked.

"Forget it," she said. "I keep my wallet and keys in my pocket. I don't know why I carry a bag that size. All I had in there was Kleenex and a couple of speeding tickets."

She bought me an ice cream to settle my stomach and gave me back to my mom in time for lunch, and that was that. She never said anything more about the incident. She's probably forgotten about it now, but I sure haven't.

CHAPTER 32

We're almost across the river when Ray gets back at me. He's not used to being laughed at—it never happens in the family. And he hates to lose. He has to even the score, even if it means cheating.

What he does, he gives a sudden jump, coming down hard. The tree trunk is thin and rotten near the far bank, and it breaks under Ray's feet. He leaps to safety. I don't. I slip on the smooth rounded trunk and go down, sliding sideways off the tree and into the water.

I bounce up as fast as I can. The river is a bit deeper here than where Ray went in—over my chest. My feet are on wobbly rocks. It's all I can do to stay upright against the fast-moving current.

"How does *that* feel?" Ray says. "I fell in, you fell in. Or do you still want to laugh at me?"

He kneels and holds out his hand, and at just that moment, I'm hit by a floating branch racing downstream—a heavy one, straight as a spear, that stabs me in the chest and knocks me off my feet. I clutch at the branch but can't catch hold. I'm carried on the current, five yards, fifteen, thirty. I come up gasping and unable to touch bottom. Ray calls something, but by now I'm too far away to hear him and moving farther.

This is a surprising development. I'm not happy about it. But, you know, I don't envy Ray. Making someone fall in the river and watching him drown—I couldn't do that. I'd rather be here. That's weird, isn't it?

Not that I'm drowning yet.

Downstream I go. The banks fly by. The river spins me around and rolls me over. Julius is like me, skinny as a flagpole and about as buoyant. I'm sinking, snatching gulps of air whenever my head gets above the surface. Rounding a bend in midstream, I bump into a section of wooden fence trim—you know the kind, with the cross hatching. I get my head and shoulders above water and draw deep breaths. I pass a family of ducks, floating calmly in a backwater by the bank. My bandana is in my eyes. I pull it off and toss it away. I'm having trouble concentrating. My thoughts drift with me, and then away from me. I think about laughing at Ray just now and about his worried face as I floated away.

I think about Nana, who used to be so sharp. The wings in the Golden Years Villa are named for trees. Different trees for different levels of need. Nana started in the Maple wing but had to move to Poplar when she needed a wheelchair. Now she's in Birch and doesn't remember anybody's name.

No one comes out of Birch.

I lose count of my breathing. In *two three* out *two*—in *one*—out—whatever. I think about how much wetter water feels when you're wearing clothes. And colder. I think about garden gnomes and cigarettes. About maple doughnuts and strollers, and hearing your best friend call you a bad name. I think about where poor Julius is while I'm him.

I don't think very long about this, because I have, like, no idea.

There's another bridge—the one by Lipton's convenience store. I've drifted a long way.

I get a sudden picture of Leon, in his coat of many colours and his sunburst hair, smiling at me. I'd like to smile back, but I can't because I'm shivering.

The river widens around the next bend. It's like a big pond. The current slows down. There's backyards on my right and a park on my left. The river laps at the top of the bank.

I see fire trucks and machines for lifting and dragging. I see men in overalls and hard hats. The junk floating downstream has piled up here and made a dam. The men are trying to un-dam the river.

The thought gets stuck in my brain. *Un-dam.*

One of the firefighters points at me, shouts something I can't hear. I know him. I can't remember his name, but something about him makes me feel bad. He splashes out to grab me. The water comes up almost to the top of his hip-waders.

CHAPTER 33

'm sitting in the front seat of a fire engine, wrapped in a thick shiny blanket and drinking hot chocolate. The heater is on full blast. Magnus's dad is sitting in the driver's seat beside me. He tells me his name and asks me mine.

"Julius," I say after a second. So many names today.

"Julius what?"

I shake my head.

"You're disoriented," he says.

"No, no, I'm fine, Mr. Quinn."

"So sorry, son, but you're not fine. You're suffering from hypothermia. Hear the siren? That's an ambulance coming to take you to the hospital."

So sorry. His wife says that all the time. Mrs. Quinn. Magnus's mom.

That's why I felt bad about Mr. Quinn—Magnus.

The fire engine is on the gravel path leading out of the kiddie park. The heater is on. Across the street and up a bit is a long building with a metal roof and a pile of snow outside the side doors. The sign on the building says Monty Loewen Memorial Arena.

You don't expect snow in September, except outside a skating rink.

I feel warm. Not just from drink. I know where the arena is, so I know where I am.

"That's Furnace Street, right?"

"Yes," says Mr. Quinn.

"So 5th Avenue is the next one over."

"Yes. Do you recognize this area, Julius? Do you play hockey, maybe? Or do you live around here?"

The siren's getting louder. I do not want to go to the hospital. I'm close to where I want to be right now. It's getting clearer with every click, every picture, that I have to get to 5th Avenue and find Gord.

My clothes are on the floor near me. I'm practically naked under the blanket. Apparently first aid for hypothermia means getting you out of everything wet. All I have on is a pair of striped underpants.

"What are you doing, Julius?" asks Mr. Quinn.

"Just grabbing my clothes. Like I said, I'm fine. My mind is clear. I'll get dressed and go."

"You're still shivering and disoriented. You don't know your name."

"But I'm okay."

"So sorry, but I can't let you. Keep your blanket on. We'll get you to the hospital in a few minutes. Say, what's that in your hand?"

Julius's water bottle is in the river, but my camera

survived the journey in the pouch of his belt. I knew it would be there.

I'm in a strange state of mind. I feel like I've passed through some kind of barrier and I'm in a new world. My day, seemingly random and frantic, has been a journey to here. Is that faith, or hypothermia?

The *SureFlash* camera is soaking wet. The green cardboard has peeled away from the frame. The counter says 9. Three shots left.

"I haven't seen one of those in a while," says Mr. Quinn. "Is it yours? Do you want me to keep it for you?"

I shake my head hard.

"That's okay. You hang onto it, then."

He smiles the way Mom smiles at Nana. A *there there* smile.

I hope the camera still works. It should work. It had better work. I'm not worried. Yes, I am.

I don't want to be Julius for the rest of my life. Ray's friend, Ray's running partner.

I want—

What do I want? To get to 5th Avenue and find Gord. And see Leon again. Just the thought of him makes me warmer inside.

CHAPTER 34

An ambulance appears, lights flashing. It rockets down the street, bumps over the curb and into the park, and skids to a halt next to our firetruck. Mr. Quinn climbs down to talk to the ambulance guys. I shiver and think about my next move.

I'm a block or two away from where I need to be. I can walk there in three minutes. But Mr. Quinn is insisting on taking me to the hospital. Which is miles away.

I won't do it. I won't go. What's Julius good at? Running. But I can't run away. I'm way too weak, and he'd catch me. I have another idea.

A pickup truck pulls into the parking lot of the arena across the street. A father and son get out. The dad hefts a hockey bag from the truck bed. The kid points excitedly and starts towards us.

I lift the wet camera to my eye.

The viewfinder is blurry. I shake the camera. Nope, still blurry. I shake again.

The kid's hair flaps in front of his face as he runs. Dad follows more slowly, carrying the hockey bag, yelling.

Ever notice the way you can go to a crowded place and keep running into the same faces? Thousands of people at Canada's Wonderland the afternoon we went last summer, but I swear I ran into this one family a dozen times, including in the bathrooms under Wonder Mountain, where the three boys were peeing in a row. This kid with the flapping hair is Greg, the one in the Red Wings jersey I saw in his driveway this morning, and then at the Cinnamon Hut, and now here. His dad is the jerk in the buzz cut who was mean to Doreen.

Greg's team must have a practice at the arena. Or else there's a tournament. I remember the sign in the Best Western, welcoming the minor atom players.

Do I want to be Greg? No. Too young. What about his dad? Or Mr. Quinn? Maybe. Whoever I choose, I have to do it fast. The ambulance guys are coming to take me away.

The viewfinder is still blurry. All I see is fuzzy moving blobs. I hold my breath and press the button.

STILL JULIUS

CHAPTER 35

Nothing happens. No click, no transformation. I still have Julius's lean arms, muscular legs, river-wrinkled fingertips. There's still a bruise in the middle of my chest, from where the tree branch hit me. Nothing continues to happen.

The picture counter still says 9. *SureFlash*? Maybe not.

I sit up straight on the cracked vinyl seat of the fire engine. My blanket drops from my shoulders to my waist.

You know what? I'm getting sick and tired of how *hard* this all is, how *complicated*, how many things go wrong. If there's a lesson I'm supposed to be learning, would somebody please tell me! Send a message. *You know you're gay. Your ex-friend's a bigot. There's other people out there for you. You're Jonah. You're lucky. You're okay.*

See? Easy. Sheesh.

I'm okay.

I shake the camera again, tighten the spool with my thumb, and now—*aha!*—the mechanism moves. There's a wheezy creaking whirr and then a click, and the number moves from 9 to 10. Yes! There's an arrow that shows you what picture number you are up to, and the arrow is definitely pointing to the 10.

But I'm still Julius.

And I've lost another picture.

What now? I stare at the stupid soggy cardboard box. I feel cheated, like my genie has changed his mind. *Did I say three wishes? Just kidding. You're done.*

My future is in my hand, and I'm afraid it's broken.

I was pretty sure of myself just a few minutes ago, and now I'm not. What happens to hope? Where does it go?

The door on my side of the fire truck swings wide open. The uniformed ambulance guy asks if I'm Julius.

The kid Greg stands away from the truck, gawking at me. His dad has a hold of the Red Wings jersey from behind and is trying to drag his son away.

"But look, Daddy! Look! That boy has no . . ."

GREG

CHAPTER 36

"...clothes!" I say.

I'm on my feet, on the ground, staring up at the fire truck. My hair is in my eyes. My shirt is bunched around my neck, because Dad is pulling me backwards.

"Whaddaya mean?" he says from behind me. "The boy in the fire truck? Whaddaya want to worry about him for, Greg?"

That's me. I'm Greg. I let Dad pull me away. I can feel my blood rushing around inside me, as if I've just eaten a big chocolate bar. Zowie! I'm back on track. The camera *does* work. Just a bit of a delay. I knew it. I knew it. I knew it. I believed it all along, even when I was doubting. I push my hair out of my eyes.

The ambulance guy helps Julius out of the fire engine. He shivers—and it's probably not just the cold. He must be scared to death. Mr. Quinn helps get him into the ambulance and waves goodbye.

Right now, I have to find Gord.

From the park side of the street, I can read the address of the house next to the arena. It's written out in fancy script over the door: *Twenty-Seven, Furnace Street.* Like I thought, I'm a corner or two away from where I want to be.

I can't just take off for 5th Avenue. Buzz-cut Dad will catch me. I'm not Julius—a relief—but I still have problems. That's been my day, hasn't it? One step forward, one step back.

So, what should I do?

The ambulance backs out of the park and speeds up Furnace Street, lights flashing. Dad throws the hockey bag over my head. It's like he's roping a steer. The strap catches on my shoulder, making me stagger. The bag hangs to my knees and weighs, like, seven hundred pounds. I'm hobbled.

"Come on, Greg. Whaddaya wasting time for? Your team's waiting for you!"

Dad grabs a corner of my bag and pulls me back through the park towards the arena. He's giving me hockey advice—telling me to do something when the other side is doing something else. I'm not listening. I've got a bigger problem than I thought.

I can't find the camera.

Yeah, maybe I could dump the bag and run away from Dad, and get to Gord's house and Leon's. Maybe. But the camera is important. It's been part of my day. It's *been* my day. I have to find it.

Dad grabs me.

"Whaddaya doing, Greg? Get your head in the game! This is your first Atom tournament."

Where's the camera? It's not in any of my pockets—not even the zippered ones. Did I drop it by the fire truck? I look over my shoulder.

"Tell me," says Dad.

"What?"

"You know what I want to hear, Greg. Tell me you're not quitting."

He leans over me, forcing me to stop and pay attention to him.

"Say it," he says. "*I won't quit.*"

What a lot of scorn Dad gets into that word. Quitting is clearly the worst thing you can do. Worse than lying or stealing or treason. I imagine a dinner table conversation.

So what did you do in school today, Greg?

Well, Dad, I cheated on a math test and pushed a teacher down the stairs, and I had to stab this kid because he looked at me funny.

Did you quit?

No, sir.

That's my boy.

"Say it now," says Dad.

"I won't quit," I say.

"Again! Say it like you mean it!"

I take a deep breath. "I. Won't. Quit."

And I do mean it.

He can hear the conviction in my voice. Satisfied, he strides ahead of me onto the street.

The hockey bag cuts into my hip and back and shoulder. What's *in* there? Pads, skates, uniform. What else? What else *could* be in there?

Oh. Maybe.

I drop the bag at the edge of the park, unzip, and there it is, perched on top of a pair of Red Wings hockey pants—a familiar rectangle covered in faded damp green cardboard. I can feel energy running out from my heart to the tips of my fingers. Relief, hope, call it what you want. This camera is my link to me.

CHAPTER 37

The houses have their lights on. The day is growing older, afternoon turning into evening. A quiet time. Smells of September—smoke, school, summer-over sadness—with a hint of mud. The sun is below the trees.

With the camera in my hand, I feel more like a *doer* and less like a *done-to-er*. I don't make the magic, but I use it. It's like surfing, I guess. I don't create the wave, but with the camera, I can ride it, instead of standing here and letting it knock me down.

Does that make sense?

I check the number at the top. Still two shots left. Shots that I will take.

"Excuse me, good neighbour," calls a voice from across the street. "Where is this house, rest place of my weary soul? Do you know this address?"

The speaker pulls up the sleeve of his colourful coat to read the writing on his arm.

Now that I have the camera, I feel pretty good. When I see who's talking, I feel even better. I run across the street, smiling wider than my face. The bare arm has *I SAVE* on it.

"Leon! It's Phil, from the police station! You called me Lucky. I told you about the weird day I'm having. You threw me this camera. This one. Remember?"

I talk really fast. There isn't much time. Dad is running towards us with a face that says trouble.

Leon's eyes are small and dark brown. He squints them even smaller, so they look like slivers of toffee or something.

"I *do* recall," he says. "The police station. And someone lucky. Was that you?"

Dad is almost here.

"Greg! Where's your hockey bag? Whaddaya DOING?"

I ignore him.

"Do you want to go home?" I say to Leon. "I'll take your picture now, and you'll wake up there. It'll be a mystery. You won't understand how you got there. Is that okay?"

For some reason, it's important that I ask permission. I haven't asked anyone else. But Leon is, well, special.

He spreads his arms. "I don't understand how I got *here*," he says.

Fair enough.

And now here's Dad, madder than a kicked beehive. He picks me up round the waist with one giant arm and strides off. I'm facing backwards.

I smile at Leon, lift the camera and press the button.

LEON

CHAPTER 38

Something looms over me. I think: *tree*. There's a banging sound off in the distance. I think: *door*. Something goes by over my head. I think: *bird*. I think: *black*. The thoughts are my own—I know birds like this. I recognize the tree. I see the arena door slam shut after Greg's dad carries him through it. But there seems to be a loose connection between noticing something and processing it.

I'm alone. I take a step, and another one, and another one. I think in individual images and words: *sidewalk, puddle, Furnace Street*. Something goes by. *Car with four doors.*

Living in Leon's body is like giving a TV interview via satellite. There's a pause between question and answer while my brain unscrambles things. It's my brain, not Leon's, but the links between brain and senses are his links, and they're a bit off.

If this is Leon's worldview, I understand why he always seems distracted.

I walk down Furnace Street and take the first cross street. The park is behind me.

In my left coat pocket is a paperback book. I don't recognize any of the words in the title except the first one, *The*. Leon's brain might get it, but mine doesn't. I put the book back. In my right coat pocket is the camera. I take it out. The arrow at the top is pointing to the number 11. One more picture left for me to take.

The first street I come to is 5th Avenue. I turn right. The first house has the number hanging from one nail. *Nine*. The next one is Seven. I'm beginning to process the world a little faster. Clouds, birds, mud. Music from an upstairs window.

I don't get to this part of town very much. The houses are big and saggy, like they're tired. The wide lawns have dandelions. The sidewalk is broken and uneven.

Another black bird flies by. Leon might have a long weird way of saying what the bird was—with feathers as black as black things and eyes even blacker than that. But I think of it as a crow.

At the bottom of the street is a blocky place with a wooden ramp to the front door. The blue van in the driveway has a licence plate with one of those wheelchair designs, so it can park anywhere. The address is on a pillar: 1 5th Avenue.

The front door opens before I knock. A familiar lady says, "Leon! Where have you been? You have been gone for over an hour. Mama is expecting you in the kitchen. You're supposed to be helping her, remember?"

I hear this almost as fast as she says it. I'm getting the hang of being Leon.

She helps me off with my coat of many colours and hangs it up. Martha, that's her name. The caring lady who came to get Leon from the police station. Underneath the coat, I'm wearing normal clothes. Leon's jeans and T-shirt could have come from my dresser at home. I transfer the disposable camera from coat pocket to pants pocket.

Martha points at a pair of slippers on the floor—mine, I guess. Some kind of plaid. I slide out of my shoes and put them on.

"Where's Gord?" I ask.

My first spoken words. Hahaha. I forgot that Leon has a Harry Potter accent.

"I want to see Gord now," I say, trying my best to pronounce the *r*.

"You have kitchen duty, Leon. Don't worry about Gord. Dinner is in a half hour, and Mama is waiting. Come with me, please."

"No!"

I surprise myself. I thought I was relaxed, ready to let the world come to me. But it seems like I want to do stuff, and do it now.

I've been shaken and rolled like dice in a board game. I've been in jail and a car crash and a flood. I'm down to one shot in the camera, and I want to find the guy who gave it to me. Now that I'm finally in his house, I'm not going to stop looking because some nice lady says so.

I hear voices in the room on the far side of the hall. I rush towards the open door.

"Gord!" I call. "Gord, are you there?"

Three kids stare at me, two from a chesterfield with cracked red leather upholstery and one from a wheelchair.

The TV is on—*Family Guy*. Lois and Stewie are fighting.

"Hi, vacuum," says a guy with four or five red blotches on his forehead and cheeks, and thick glasses.

The girl beside him on the couch tells him to shut up.

"What do you think, Leon?" says the girl in the wheelchair, holding out her arms, like, *ta da*. "Do you like?"

I don't know what she's talking about.

They're all wearing plaid slippers. Green, blue, red. This is an orderly house. I bet the toothbrushes and towels are colour-coded too.

"Any of you seen Gord?" I ask.

The two girls shake their heads. The pimply guy says, "Hi, elbow." His glasses are held on with a strap.

On TV, Stewie leaps on his mom and throws her against the wall.

I go back to the hall. Martha tells me again that I am on kitchen duty. I head up the stairs. She sighs after me. The second floor has a centre hall with rooms off it. Three doors are open, revealing a couple of empty bedrooms—one of which is so book-cluttered it has to be Leon's—and a games room, where a bald guy is killing zombies and doesn't know anything about Gord.

The fourth door is closed. I knock. A girl's voice tells me to come in.

She's sitting in a rocking chair with a book in her lap. I see this in the light from the hall. The room itself is dark.

She turns calmly towards me. She's my age, more or less. Why would she choose to read in a darkened room? How can she even do it?

184

"Have you seen Gord?" I ask her. "It's important."

She laughs—a genuine one. There's a white cane leaning on the dresser. I feel pretty foolish.

"I mean, do you know where he is?"

"No, sorry," she says.

"Leon!" calls Martha. "Come out of Harriet's room."

"Are you okay, Leon?" she says. "You don't sound exactly like yourself."

Funny what some people can hear.

CHAPTER 39

Martha follows me up a steep set of stairs to the third floor, talking about following rules and learning to be with others.

"What's *wrong* with you, Leon?" she says. "Getting lost last night was bad enough, and now this strange obsession about Gord. Harriet's right. You're not yourself."

We get to the top of the stairs in a little square hall. Dark wood, dimness and dust. Martha points at the closed door in front of me.

"Go on," she says. "Check his room. You've checked everywhere else."

I throw open the door and turn on the light. The room's practically empty. An iron bed frame with a thin mattress, a dresser, and an empty wastebasket.

"Satisfied now, Leon? Will you go downstairs and help Mama?"

"When's he coming back?"

Martha sighs. I'm a particularly sharp stone in her shoe full of stones.

"You know Gord. He comes and goes."

Downstairs, the kitchen has a wide door that swings open when you push it. Makes me stop and stare. Something I recognize.

"You know, *my* house has a kitchen door just like this one," I say.

"Yes, Leon. Just like this one. In fact it *is* this one. This is your house."

I laugh. She's got me. But in fact, my house has a heavy white swinging kitchen door a whole lot like this one. Ray usually shoulders through it like a running back. Mom likes to kick it open and stand there laughing, *haw haw haw*.

The door opens towards me now, releasing a billow of steam and revealing a wide, warm, comfortable woman. She fills the doorway and her clothes—fills them to the brim. She reminds me of a toasted bun—round, soft, sweet. My worry and anger disappear. She absorbs the bad feelings.

"Leon!"

Face as big and round as a soccer ball, her happiness inflating it full. Steam billows out from the kitchen and surrounds her.

"Hello, Mama. Here's Leon at last," says Martha.

"I thought I heard him talking," she cries. "Leon, honey, where've you been? There's corn to shuck."

The kitchen's warm and full of good smells. A safe place. Mama's safe too. I can tell her anything. I come right out with the truth, surprising myself.

"I'm not really Leon," I say.

She nods. "I know."

"You do?"

She stands in front of the stove, stirring. I smell garlic and tomato and something spicy. Steam vents from the pots. Mama exists in a cloud.

"You're always someone else," she says. "You get talking, and you turn into all sorts of people."

"I mean it," I say. "I'm not Leon. I'm a different boy."

"Usually you're not a boy," says Mama. "Usually you're a prince or a wizard or a gravedigger or something. Remember when you were those two old men? Look with your ears, the crazy one said to the blind one. Change places and handy dandy. You made me laugh, all right."

She hands me a big bag from the No Frills store. "But you still have a job to do. Dinner's in fifteen minutes."

"I want to see Gord," I say.

"Why?"

I don't want to lie to Mama, but no kind of truth is going to make sense. I'm alone on a vast plain of uncertainty. The amount I don't know stretches away from me in all directions.

"He can help me," I say finally.

Mama smiles like we're sharing a secret.

"Sure he can," she says. "He'll be around. You know him. He comes and goes."

"But I want—"

She pushes me over to a plastic-topped table by the window. "Put the husks in the compost bag."

Mindless tasks can be soothing. While I'm getting the corn ready, I don't worry about what I'm going to do if I can't find Gord.

The door swings open, and the girl in the wheelchair rolls over to the counter.

"Can you help me reach the glasses, Leon?" she asks.

Her legs look like sticks, and one foot is bent inwards. I wonder if she bumps herself up and down stairs or if someone carries her.

"There's this real cute guy in a car commercial," she says, as I stack the glasses in her lap. "He comes out of the ocean in a teeny bathing suit. Water drips off him, and, well, I thought of you. You want me to call you next time the commercial is on?"

"Uh, thanks," I say.

I try to seem cool, but inside I am kind of shouting. She knows about Leon. Maybe everyone does.

"Thanks," I say again.

My inside shouting doesn't last for long. People know about me—about Leon. That's great, but it's not an explosion. It's more like, okay, fine, now what?

The dinner table seats eight comfortably. Martha sits at the head, with her hands in her lap and her back straight. Blind Harriet's across from me, chatting to the girl in the wheelchair. The pimply kid with the glasses slips into the seat on the other side of her.

"Hi, popcorn," he says to the table in general.

The tough girl on my left rolls her eyes.

On the other side of me is the bald guy with the cutthroat tattoo. Gord isn't here. There's no grown man here.

I'm not hungry, but I am something. Some other kind of empty. Nothing to do with the time of day.

Mama serves us from a rolling cart and sits at the bottom of the table, and then we all hold hands and say grace. I don't know these words. I move my lips and go *blah blah blah* under my breath. Dinner is stew in a red sauce. Meat and onions and peppers and peas, with rice underneath. The corn—my corn—is on the side.

When dinner's over, we pass our plates to Celeste, the girl in the wheelchair, and she stacks them onto the rolling trolley.

Mama's size and comfort surround us all. It's like being in a steamy shower. On the wall behind her is a framed crayon picture, a house and sun and three figures—Mommy and Daddy and Me. I remember the sergeant saying this was a place for at-risk youth. I hope the picture is old, and that whoever drew it left years ago and is now happy somewhere.

"Songs?" the bald guy says to me. "You know any songs?"

He licks small pieces of corn off his lips, his tattoo sawing up and down on his throat when he swallows.

"Yes, Leon. How about one of your songs? Or a recitation," says Harriet from across the table. "If you're up to it, that is."

Everyone looks at me expectantly. The light from the chandelier flashes off the *Hi, popcorn* kid's glasses.

Mama nods encouragement. "*You* know. What we were talking about before dinner in the kitchen."

"Change places and handy dandy?"

"Or a song." Her cheeks pleat in a smile.

The bald guy pounds on the table. "Song song song!" he cries, and others join in.

I remember the Christmas when Nana made Ray sing. That was the year she knitted us sweaters for presents—nubby bumpy colourful things. Mine had moons and stars on it. Ray laughed and said my sweater was girly. I didn't know what to say, because I liked it, so I didn't say anything. Ray laughed some more, and finally Mom told him to stop.

A little later, Nana called Ray over to her chair.

"Your mother tells me you sang a carol at the school concert, Raymond. Sang it beautifully," she said. "Why don't you stand there beside the tree and sing it for me now? Please, Raymond—sing for your nana."

I knew Ray would rather swallow a bug than sing, but Mom was there, nodding amid the wrapping paper, so he cleared his throat and started in, sensitive as a sunburn. *"Good King Wenceslas looked out, On the feast of Stephen . . ."*

Nana made him sing all the verses, beating time on the arm of her chair. I watched from the corner of the living room in a kind of trance. So complete was my brother's humiliation that I didn't want to miss a note.

At the end, Nana turned to me and winked. And I realized in a flash that she had staged this whole thing—this miracle— for me, because Ray had been mean about my present.

Cutlery is bouncing as everyone pounds the table, and the room echoes. I'm embarrassed, and I have no idea what to sing, but this is not the worst moment of my day. They aren't being mean. They like Leon.

I do too. I wish I could be here listening to him.

"Song song song!"

I stand up and clear my throat, and the chanting dies away. I look down at my hands—nice-looking ones, clean, with long fingers and squared finger-ends.

I don't know any of that handy dandy stuff. I'm me, not Leon. I open my *self*—heart and mind and all—to the universe. And this is what comes out.

> *"Two of us so much in love,*
> *Higher than the stars above,*
> *You're all that I'm thinking of,*
> *Baby..."*

I didn't know I was paying attention to the words in the mall, but there they are. This is the song the universe sends me. Funny old universe.

You know, I sound pretty good. When I was Magnus, I could jump. As Dan'l, I could drive. As Julius, I could run. And as Leon, I can sing.

Celeste smiles across the table at me. The kid with the glasses sits totally still, eyes fixed on me. I'm working to remember the next verse.

> *"You're the only one I see,*
> *Floating to eternity,*
> *Me and you and you and me,*

Baby.
I need you, I need you, Oh, how I need you."

That's all the words I have, so I sit down. Harriet thanks me gravely. My bald neighbour is weeping openly. And I realize I'm having a pretty good time.

Mama goes to the kitchen and comes back with a cake and a stack of small plates on the rolling cart. Martha follows, leading a shy guy with dripping hands, damp hair pushed away from his face, and a clean *I ♥ NY* sweatshirt that's too big for him. Martha takes her place at the head of the table and frowns at me, like, *Now are you happy?*

Mama cuts the cake. The new arrival hands out the plates, ducking his head each time he serves someone.

"For you," he says to Celeste. "For you," to the tough girl on my left.

It's my turn. I hold out my hands.

"For *you*."

"Hi, Gord," I say.

His eyes—those amazing eyes with the gold flecks—light right up.

"Hiya, Lucky!" he says. "You made it. Wonderful."

My heart is doing a little syncopated thing. *Ka-dunt dunt.* I feel it in there, banging away.

"I have to talk to you," I say.

He hands his last plate to the bald guy, who starts eating while the plate is still in the air. His tattoo jumps up and down when he swallows.

Mama gets to her feet and pushes Gord ahead of her. "He'll eat in the kitchen," she tells Martha.

"I have to talk to him."

"Sure," says Mama. "But let him eat first."

Martha tells me what happened to Gord. "Mall security found him in the Dumpster and called the police," she says. "Did you know he was in trouble, Leon? Is that why you went looking for him all over the house?"

I shake my head. I wonder if the mall security was Mary Lee.

Celeste leans over the table and whispers my name. "Gord called you lucky," she says. "Why? Why did he do that?" She's laughing at me.

"That's the question," I say.

The meal's over. Julia, the tough girl, comes over to say that my song sucked. I agree with her. She frowns and lets the kid with the glasses lead her away.

Ka-dunt dunt, goes my heart. *Ka-dunt dunt. Ka-dunt dunt.*

CHAPTER 40

Gord sits at the table where I shucked the corn. The dishes are piled by the sink. Mama, surrounded by suds and steam, is washing up.

I take the other seat at the table. "Leon told me you lived here," I say to Gord. "But when I arrived, you weren't around."

He chews carefully, like he suspects that there's a bone in there. He doesn't seem surprised that I talk about Leon in Leon's voice, wearing Leon's face. He knows I'm someone else.

"They found you in the Dumpster, eh?" I say. "Sounds yucky."

"I've been worse places."

I take the camera out of my pocket and put it on the table in front of him. He looks from it up at me. His eyes sparkle.

"Twelve wishes," he says. "Twelve chances."

"You remember that?"

"Why not? It was only this morning. And did the camera work?"

What does he mean, *did it work*? He knows I'm not Leon. He knows the camera worked.

Gord chews, swallows. Now that I've found him and the threads of the day are twisting themselves together, I feel nervous. Like, what did I miss? Like, what now?

"I tried to take Magnus's picture again," I say. "I didn't know the rules—that you could only become someone else once. I wasted a couple of shots."

Gord pushes away his empty dinner plate and reaches for the piece of cake Mama has cut for him. I watch him eat, and find that I am clenching and unclenching my hands all the time.

"There's one shot left," I say. "What then? What happens to Leon? To me? Will I wake up at home, or in some mental hospital? Or am I—?"

It just occurred to me. Holy crap. All the stories I've read. All the movies. Of course, there's an easy explanation for what's going on today.

"Am I dead?"

Gord looks up from his cake.

"I don't *feel* dead," I say.

"Good."

"Mind you, I'm Leon now, so I don't know about me. Me Jonah, I mean. But I *think* like me, and I don't think I'm dead. Maybe I'm just crazy."

That's not as bad as being dead.

"Do you feel crazy?" Gord asks.

"Sort of."

The overhead light catches his eyes, making them shimmer. It's like watching sunlight on water.

"Good," he says.

"Is it?"

Is it good to feel crazy? To feel you don't fit, that you don't know what's going to happen, that you can't understand anything, not even yourself? Gord must know what that's like, wandering around town talking to himself. I've been happy today, and scared, and mad. I've been hopeful and sad. I've been male and female, young and old, guilty and innocent, lost and found. Mostly lost. And all those people were me. There were times I felt that I was being looked after, part of a plan—and then the very next moment, my life was in danger.

Gord smiles, puts the camera in his pants pocket. "So it worked," he says.

He gives his empty plates to Mama to wash, picks up two drying towels and tosses one to me.

"Thanks, you two," says Mama.

After the dishes are done, we change our slippers for shoes and go out into the backyard to dump the corn husks into the compost pile. The sky is grey. Bats and bugs are out there squeaking and buzzing. The air smells of rain past and more to come. A couple of stars are out. I can't decide if they look lonely or if they just don't care.

Light streams from the kitchen across the backyard. I hear a burst of laughter from somewhere, and a low booming sound that could be the lake. We collect bird feeders from around the yard, refill them from a bag of seed we find in the tool shed, and hang them up again.

Gord stands in the middle of the yard, puts his arms out, and begins spinning. I watch him out of the corner of my eye, the way you'd watch someone who, for no reason, started to break dance or do push-ups.

I wish I was wearing something warmer than a T-shirt. I find myself thinking of Leon's coat. A nice thought—Leon, his smile, and his random way of talking. Funny thought, of course, since I'm him.

A puff of wind crosses the yard, ruffling the low, rounded shrub beside me into a cheerleader's pompom. Suddenly I smell my bedroom. Weird, eh? You know how your pyjamas get after you've worn them a few days? Comfortable, sweet, tired, familiar. I guess they smell like you. Anyway, that's what I get now. My pyjamas with the stripes and drawstring. I can practically see my rumpled bed, my rag rug, my bookshelf, my desk with my laptop on it, and the drawer with my tube of skin cream. My stuff.

Gord stops spinning.

"Now," he says, and he leads the way back into the house.

CHAPTER 41

Martha's waiting for us in the downstairs bathroom. She hands me a plastic cup with two pills in it. The room is huge—two sinks and two toilet stalls. A door wide enough for the wheelchair. And, as I guessed, cubbies with towels and toothbrushes.

I don't really want to take the pills, but they are Leon's and I am him. They are part of today. I drink some water to help them down.

"You guys wash up, then go the TV room and let the girls have a turn in here," says Martha.

Gord washes his hands. There's a strong smell of lemon. He tosses the soap into my sink so I can wash too.

He's taken the camera from his pocket. It sits on the counter between the two sinks. The green cardboard is falling off the plastic frame. The lens points at me.

Martha leaves the door open when she goes.

For good or bad, for whatever today is about, this is it. I wonder if Gord will disappear, the way he did at the mall.

He comes and goes. I'm scared but excited. Not like at Christmas, more like when I'm on the high diving board. Yeah.

"Wash up," he says.

I pick up the wet soap and drop it in surprise. It looks like a typical yellow bar with bubbles of lather, but there's a definite buzzing feeling in my palm. I remember washing in the women's bathroom at the mall. The soap there gave me the same feeling.

I tell Gord the soap stings. He nods.

"Cleans deep," he says.

High diving board. But before I jump, I have a question. It's kind of been in the background all day.

"Why me?" I ask.

"Why—?"

"*For you*, you said. *For you, for you, for you*. What's so special about me? Why am I the only one who has these weird things happen to him? Is it because I'm gay? Is that it?"

"Are you? Who says you are?"

Gord puts his head on one side. The golden flecks in his eyes jump like sparks in a bonfire.

"Am I gay?" I say. "Yeah. I think so. Yeah, I am." All the people I got to be today—cool ones and weirdos, boys and girls, old people and babies—I was always me, and I was always gay.

He smiles. "I meant, who says you're the only special one?"

I'm starting to feel woozy. The pills, I guess. I pick up the soap and hang on this time. It's sting-y but in a not-bad way.

You know how spicy food tastes? Like that, only in my hands instead of my mouth. They sure do come up clean. Fingertips especially—as if whole layers of skin are gone. When I wash my face, the water pouring down the sink is dark brown. I must be dirtier than I thought.

I thought I was used to being Leon, but now I get that time delay again—the pause between seeing and knowing. I lift my head and think, a second later, *Horror movie.*

I'm dissolving. Forehead, nose, cheeks, chin are dripping off me. It's like my face is made of mud, and I'm flushing it away. No wonder the water is filthy.

I hear a noise and think, *Scream.* That'll be me. Under Leon's face, behind the ripped curtain of flesh, is another face, a different set of features.

"Again," says Gord.

I've jumped off the high board. Too late to go back. I lather up and scrub with all my force. Feels like I'm washing in electricity. But the rinse water is coming clean at last. I'm so dizzy I can barely stand. Who's that staring out from the mirror? The bathroom whirls.

Gord hands me the camera. "Now, Lucky!"

I aim at the face in the mirror. I think, *me.* And I think, *okay.*

I press the button, and my index finger takes the rest of me with it, down, down, down. Darkness rushes towards me like water from a burst dam.

LUCKY ME

CHAPTER 42

I'm lying on the cold wet floor. I prop myself up on one elbow. The bathroom revolves a quarter turn or so, and a voice intones from above me.

"He starts, he moves, he seems to feel, the thrill of life along his keel."

Familiar voice. I look up. Leon's staring down at me, with his hurricane hair and his tiny raisin eyes.

"Leon!" I say. "You're not me. I mean, I'm not you." That doesn't sound right. "I mean, you're you."

That doesn't sound right either.

"I think so," he says. "Though I can never be sure."

I work myself into a sitting position, leaning against the bathroom wall. Still a little woozy. I tell Leon it's great to see him.

"So we're friends?" he says. "Good friends? I doubt it not, but I am surprised. Because till now I never saw your face."

"I told you my story," I say. "And you saved me. But you never met me looking like this."

He's standing where Gord was, over by the far sink. He's holding a towel, like Gord was. And he's wearing the *I ♥ NY* sweatshirt. But if I used to be him, and if *he* took Gord's place, then who am I now?

How can you be full of hope and fear at the same time? But I am. Full of faith. And doubt. So often today I wanted to be someone else, and now—well, it's funny, like I said.

Speaking of hope, it's good to see Leon. He's really got something.

Mind you, he is a little older than I am. Three years? I'm thirteen and he's at least sixteen. Maybe more than three years.

That's older.

Mama leans into the open doorway.

"I heard shouting," she says. "How are you, Leon?"

"I humbly thank you, well well well."

"Where's Gord? Why are you wearing his shirt—and—and—who are *you*?"

She doesn't frown—I don't know if she can. She's warm and welcoming. She really wants to know who I am.

So do I.

With my back against the wall, I push myself into a standing position and lean forward. There I am in the mirror, just like this morning and yesterday and the day before and all the other days. My face. Mine, from the wavy messy still-damp hair to the freckles on the bridge of my nose. My greyish watery eyes with the turned-down corners.

I'm me.

I feel like crying. You know how it is when the firefighters arrive in time to save the kid trapped in the burning house, and the music soars, and tears begin to prickle behind your eyelids? And you feel stupid for crying because it's only a movie? Like that.

And you know why I'm so happy to see myself after a whole day away? It's because this is who I am. This guy. It's the *honesty* that gets me. Go ahead—laugh. I don't blame you. I'd laugh myself if I wasn't choking up.

"I'm a friend of Leon's," I say. "My name is Jonah. He calls me Lucky."

Wouldn't you know it, my voice leaps up on the name. Luck-*ee!* Puberty is a booby trap marathon.

I clear my throat and go on quickly. "You must be Mama. Leon's told me about you."

I can see the questions in her eyes. How'd I get in her house? How come she's never seen me before?

"He really a friend of yours?" she asks Leon.

"Oh yes." He stares at me. "Indeed. And Lucky *was* your name. You told me sad stories, how you were first a man, and then a maid. I do remember all this, and feel't and see't, and 'tis wonder that enwraps me thus. But," he adds in a whisper, "you looked different."

Mama offers her hand. Mine disappears into it.

"So where's Gord?" she asks.

I have no idea. Like, none.

"You know him. He comes and goes," I say.

Mama opens her mouth like there's something else she wants to say, but she doesn't say it. She walks away.

I'm wearing my own clothes—the same ones I had on when I was watching Magnus play basketball. Which makes sense, I guess. I find the pack of gum in my pocket. I take a piece and offer one to Leon.

"Where've you been the last few hours?" I ask. "Do you remember? Or did you just *wake up* in the bathroom? Like out of a deep sleep?"

He chews carefully.

"My days are full of waking up, and being surprised at where I am," he says. "I once was lost, and now am found. Wherever I was, I am home again."

The camera's not in my pockets. I tell Leon about it. We search the bathroom together, but it's not there.

"Perhaps it vanished," he says. "Isn't that what magic things do?"

"I've had it all day," I say. "It's the same one you threw me in jail, remember? The same one I took your picture with outside the arena."

"These things finish." says Leon.

"You mean my magic day is over? Well, this is the real me. No magic now."

I wonder though. Leon is wearing Gord's sweatshirt, and Gord is who knows where, and what's that if not magic?

Leon's a little taller than me. His chin sticks out a little to the side. His cheekbones have a light dust of hair on them. Huh. He's staring at my face too. There's something between us. Does he feel it? Does he understand it?

"Jonah," he says. "And that's who you really are."

"It is."

"You're sure."

"Yeah," I say.

"And what do you want to do now, Jonah?"

There's a bunch of things I could say to that. *I want to be your friend. I want to hang out. I want to sit beside you and watch that car ad Julia was talking about—the one with the hot guy. I want to— I want to—*

"I wish I knew," I say.

He nods. "What is the end of study? Why, that to know which else we should not know."

He reaches for my hand. Squeezes. It's nice.

"Come back and see me sometime," he says.

CHAPTER 43

We go to the front hall, Leon in his slippers and me in the skate shoes I put on this morning when I left my house. He starts to call me Lucky, catches himself, and changes it to Jonah. I tell him it's okay. I feel pretty lucky. We smile.

My phone's in my pocket. No missed calls, no messages. No surprise.

I take a photo of the two of us together. My first selfie. I have to say, there's a moment when I wonder what's going to happen when the light flashes, but everything works fine, and there he is looking puzzled and kind of adorable on my phone.

Adorable? A guy? Whatever. There's no adorable girls on my phone yet. Maybe there never will be.

Martha helps Harriet downstairs, stops at the sight of us, and asks Leon why he's wearing Gord's sweatshirt.

"I bought it for *him*, Leon, not you," she says. "He doesn't have any sweatshirts. Where is he?"

"That's a mystery—like all Gord's wisdom."

"Leon, it *is* you!" says the blind girl. "You sound more like yourself than you did at dinner." She feels her way into the bathroom and closes the door.

"And who are you?" Martha asks me.

Leon does the introductions. When I say I'm heading home, she offers to drive me. She's on her way to pick up a prescription, she says, and it'll be no trouble. She checks on Harriet. Leon and I are alone for a moment to say goodbye. I'm afraid he's going to hug me, and then I'm afraid he's not. Then Martha comes back.

In the club van, I sit in the front seat beside her. She steers casually, one hand on the wheel, the other playing with the radio. She says she's pleased that Leon has found a friend close to his own age.

"He doesn't relate easily to his peers," she says.

We head up 5th Avenue past King Street, with the river and downtown on our left. The van smells of food and sweat, and of the differentness of not belonging. I can imagine Leon riding in it. And all the rest of them.

The clock tower in Victoria Hall strikes the hour. The local news comes on the radio. The announcer puts on her concerned voice.

"*Our lead story deals with the unexpected outbreak of youth violence in Dresden today. An incident in the mall this morning resulted in assault and weapons charges against an unnamed teen. Later, a high-speed police chase led to a dramatic showdown in the north end. Arrests have been made in a car theft ring. . . .*"

Martha sighs at what the town is coming to. I think about

being all of those youths in the news today. But they don't hold me. It's like they were leading me to where I am, who I am now.

So I'm me, Jonah, and I'm okay with that. And I seem to be gay, and I'm okay with that too. What do I want to do now?

I don't know.

One thing for sure—tomorrow will be different from today. I guess it always is, isn't it? But I mean really different.

I'm still daydreaming when Martha pulls into the midtown plaza. We park in front of the pharmacy. There's also a gas station, a dry cleaner, and a trophy store where they engrave plaques and cups. (Every family room I've ever been in has something from Glen's Trophy.) Martha says she'll just be a minute, but I'm already sliding out of the van and dropping to the pavement.

I tell her I can walk home from here.

"But you live over by Burnham Street."

"There's something I want to do first. Thanks for the lift."

"You aren't dressed warmly enough," she calls after me as I run towards the gas station where Magnus is filling his mom's gas tank.

"You aren't dressed warmly enough," she calls after me as I run towards the gas station. Mrs. Quinn is filling her car at the near pump. Magnus comes out of the store with a cup of coffee, a bag of chips, and a Snickers.

I've been thinking about him. What to do, what to say. I don't have a plan, but I can't pretend today didn't happen.

The Econo-Gas lights are bright, but not as bright as Magnus's face when I run up to him.

"Jonah! Hi! Great to see you!"

I can't think what to say.

"Where you been all day?" he asks. "You disappeared after the basketball game. Lisa and I missed you." He gestures at the car. There's Lisa in the back seat, talking on her phone.

"Did you? Did you really?"

"Yeah. Course I did!"

His happiness is genuine, hard to resist. His face is lit up because of me. I want to hate him but I can't. No, that's not true. I don't even *want* to hate him. But he was mean to me. But he didn't know it. But—but—

What a mess.

I can't forget what he called me, and I can't decide what to do about it. Apart from kicking him, I mean. I've already done that. Maybe I won't do anything now. But if there's an opportunity tomorrow or next week, I'll—I don't know.

Would he like me if he *knew* about me? Probably not. But would I want that guy for a friend?

One thing—I don't want to kiss him. Maybe I used to, and I'm not sorry I did, but not now.

"You don't really know me, do you," I say.

"What? Course I do."

Martha toots her horn at me, driving away from the pharmacy. I wave.

This would be the moment for me to come out to Magnus. The two of us talking quietly together. So why don't I? Why don't I just say it? Because he'll be angry, embarrassed? Nope. It's not about him. It's me. I wanted to see him and talk to him, now that I'm clear about who I am. I've done that. It's enough for now.

And then I surprise myself.

"No you don't," I say. "You don't know the first thing about me. I'm gay."

Like a piece of toast, or a joke snake, or a baby, the words pop out. I didn't intend to say it. But I have.

Magnus's mouth falls open. He may be thinking a cow flew by. He doesn't say anything. I can think of a few things. *Wanna call me a name?* I could say. *And by the way, you're a jerk*, I could say. But I don't. I face him, hands at my sides, looking dumb.

Say, is *this* the moment I've been leading up to all day—coming out to my old best friend? I can't help thinking there should be more drama to it.

Probably the big moments in your life go by before you even know they're there.

The hose kicks shut when the tank is full, and the weird little spell is broken. Mrs. Quinn hangs up the nozzle, screws on the gas cap, smiles at me.

"Why, hello, Jonah," she says. "Fancy meeting you here."

"Fancy," I say.

Magnus walks over holding out the coffee cup. His mom takes it and steps in something yucky. Gum, or worse. She drags her shoe along the ground to scrape the something off. Coffee spills.

"Uh-oh," I say. "Now that stuff's stuck to your shoe. You'll get it all over the pedals when you drive. Those are nice shoes too. And there's coffee on your pants. Poor you."

She looks like she wants to scream.

Lisa is still on her phone—the one with the picture of Magnus. To think that I was once inside her clothes. Wow. I knock on the window to get her attention and shoot her with my finger. She smiles back uncertainly.

"Well, I should be going," I say. "Don't offer me a lift. I feel like running." I take a deep breath. "Gasoline is a clean smell, isn't it?"

Magnus finally shuts his mouth. All this time he has not said a thing.

There's a big old moon rising behind the cashier's hut.

CHAPTER 44

The light's red at George Street and University. I make a sudden decision, turn left. Golden Years Villa is on the next block. The lady at the desk looks sad, like they always do when you say you're visiting someone in Birch.

There's a coded lock on the door to the wing. They don't want the Birchers getting out. I don't know why I'm here, except that I'm still getting over my last half hour—coming back to myself after most of a day away—and I don't want to go home yet. I punch the Birch security code and let myself in. The Birch nurse nods hello over an armful of sheets.

Nana's room is down the hall on the left. She's got the bed cranked so she can sleep sitting up. She's having trouble breathing these days.

"Hello, Nana," I say.

She opens one eye and says hello back with a bit of a frown.

"Who are you?" she asks. Before I can answer, she asks if I like her new butterflies. I say I do. She frowns again.

"I mean curtains," she says.

"Yes," I say.

I sit in the chair beside her bed, and we chat for a moment about the weather today, which was nice, and dinner, which was awful, and the man next door, who has two heads—that's what Nana says, anyway.

I ask her if she wants something to drink. She doesn't answer right away. Then she says her purse is dry.

I nod.

"I mean my mouth," she says.

"Would you like some water?"

I hold out her cup with the bendy straw.

She sips.

We have the same chat about dinner all over again. This is the part where Mom gets sad, but I don't mind repeating myself. Nana and I agree again that vanilla pudding is enough to make you sick.

I ask if she remembers the day at the fair when I threw up in her purse. "It was cool of you to let me do that," I say.

She asks if I have seen the man next door. "He has two heads, you know."

"Wow, really," I say.

The nurse comes in to tell me that visiting hours are almost over. I stand up. Nana lifts her hand to wave good-bye, and something happens to her eyes—or maybe behind her eyes.

"I know you," she says, in a different voice. "I'd know you anywhere. You're Jonah."

"Yes. Yes, I am."

I go over and take her hand. "It's great to see you, Nana."

She blinks a few times. Like I said, something is going on in there, her mind trying to find traction on an icy road. Her hand feels like polished wood. Her hair hangs in white wisps.

I bend low. "I want to show you something," I say.

I take out my phone, find my photo, and show her.

"Who's that?" she says. "He's cute."

"That," I whisper, "is my friend Leon. Kind of a crush."

She doesn't say anything for a second, and then she gives my arm a little squeeze. "I wondered," she says, nodding wisely.

What's this—she wondered about me maybe liking guys? I'm surprised. I mean, even *I* didn't know.

"What made you wonder?" I ask.

"And then today I saw," she says. "No more wondering. It's clear. One head on his neck and the other one growing out of his shoulders. Right here." She points at the join in her neck. "He walked past my door eating two chocolate bars at once."

Ah, Nana.

I give her a kiss goodbye.

The nurse walks me out of Birch. "That was amazing," she says. "She never recognizes anyone, but she sure knew you. You must have a strong personality."

"Oh, yeah," I said.

There's a mirror in the lobby of the villa. Mom always checks it on her way out, to make sure she's wiped away tears. I catch sight of myself, stop, and look closer.

I didn't notice in the bathroom with Leon. I guess I was too busy being thankful. But it strikes me now—my left cheek is clean. Totally clean. That painful bright red zit from this morning is gone. There's nothing left. It's like it was never there.

This is not the strangest thing that happened to me today. But it's another strange thing.

Know what I'm sorry about? Well, sure, lots of things, but walking down University Street to Burnham, I'm sorry I never thanked Gord. I've no idea where he is right now or what he actually *did* today. I know lots I didn't know this morning, but there's way more I can't even guess at. *Who says you're the only special one?* Still, I'm sorry. Next time I see him around, I'll have to remember to say thank you. If he has no idea what I'm talking about, that'll be fine.

On an impulse, I check my phone. Somehow I feel that Gord could get in touch with me anytime he wants.

No texts, no missed calls. Course not.

The photo of Leon and me makes me smile.

Turn onto Burnham, head for home. And who's going to be there? Ray.

That might have been the hardest thing, today—meeting Ray. That was a kind of turning point. Not being my brother is important to me. I can't be in his skin. I can share lives with old men and grumpy women, criminals and little babies, but not my brother.

I'm good with that.

Actually, I'm pretty good with most of what I found out today. Everyone has troubles. You're going to care more about yours than anyone else's. Which makes sense, since you can't be anyone but yourself. That's true for sure—no matter who I looked like today, I was Jonah inside.

Being gay—well, that's who I am. It's my problem. It shouldn't be a problem, but it is. Life's harder when you're different and people don't like your *kind* of different.

A whole lot of them. And you thought some of them were your friends.

I'm not looking forward to coming out, but it'll happen. It's already started. I'm not scared of Magnus—I'm mad and sad. And Ray?

Well, I can always throw a wet scarf at him.

The full moon rides like a pumpkin coach out of the shade trees on my left. Soft, rounded, and deeply knowing, in a night of black velvet shot with holes of light. My breath catches in my throat. For this moment, I'm sure it's all within reach, that I can pull down the sky and wrap it round me like a blanket. I'm full of feeling, happy and sad and hopeful and everything.

I start to run fast as I can.

ACKNOWLEDGEMENTS

This book began as a crazy adventure and became a journey that is, I hope, funny and moving and true. *Funny*, or not, is mostly me. Everything else I had help with. *Journey* is thanks to my editor, Hadley Dyer, whose sense of plot and character arc kept me on track. *Moving* and *true* come from the stories, drinks, tears, and laughter of friends who've been on the journey themselves. I am grateful to Allyson Latta for her attention to pace, and to Mackenzie Polack for pointing out a couple of places where Jonah and I got lost. As always, the sales and marketing teams—Hilary McMahon for me, and various gals and guys for HarperCollins—have my sincere thanks and fervent (oh! so fervent) best wishes.